THE STATION
SEWING CIRCLE

Lou Lewis

Published by
Llyfrau Cambria Books, Wales, United Kingdom.
Cambria Books is a division of
Cambria Publishing Ltd.
Discover our other books at: www.cambriabooks.co.uk

Men can but dream
without women with Vision.

The Tales

The Circle Members
Their Significant Relationship

Bessie the Law — Wife of Police Sergeant Evans

Bron the Books — Town Librarian

Megan the Signals — Wife of Railway Signalman

Myvvi the Dead — Wife of Undertaker

Maria from Milan — Wife of Milkman

Auntie Sian — Auntie of Blacksmith

Maggie the Shop — Wife of Local Grocer

Beryl the Will — Wife of Town Solicitor

Glenys the Coal — Wife of Coal Merchant

Penny the Photo — Assistant to Town Photographer

Carol from Chapel — Wife of Baptist Minister

Florrie the Fire — Fire Station Clerk

Joan the Tip — Wife of Dustbin Lorry Driver

A Tidy Town Indeed – *Bessie the Law*

I brought the official gathering of the Station Road Sewing Circle to a close. I could sense a distinct air of anticipation flowing into St Michael's church hall, where my weekly meeting took place with twelve other ladies. Each of us in turn had publicly declared our dedicated interest in knitting, needlework and all things stitched. Nothing could be further from the truth.

I carried my tally, Bessie the Law, with considerable pride due to my husband Sergeant Evans being the town's sole policeman. I was unanimously appointed to the chair of our exclusive sewing club, which is intent on keeping the people of Pembroke safe in their beds, flowers in every window box and the streets clear of litter. It was no small measure that our town had earned the Welcome to West Wales award for the last three years.

Two aspects of our work, conducted in secret mind you, ensured that our neighbourly mission was achieved. The thirteen of us were all well informed and as with any covert service we had the best intelligence network ably supported by many other women of the town going about their daily collection of other people's business. Gossip on doorsteps, overheard news on the bus and waiting in queues at the shops were our main sources of information. Not much went on in Pembroke that escaped us! The other reason for our continued influence on the well-being of the town was that our respective husbands had no inkling at all that most of our Circle's efforts were conducted through them after we had sown the ideas into their heads. We were more of a sowing than a stitching club you see.

I stood up and tugged at my now snug but still fashionable two-piece suit. "My husband Sergeant Evans was conducting his first patrol of the day, which you early birds will know, he completes before breakfast every morning. He came upon a sight which would indeed not be pleasant to our eyes and would certainly cause consternation within the ranks of the Welcome to West Wales judges."

I noticed Joan the Tip lean towards her neighbour in the circle and mumble. "Not another litter pick I hope, I have enough to do with four children leaving a trail of destruction at home."

"Not quite," I responded in my official voice. "I'm glad that you've spoken up girl because the matter will have to be dealt with through your husband who drives the dustbin lorry."

Joan was quick to defend her husband's reputation for street cleaning. "You can't help having the odd bit of spillage, not to mention the foxes who come down at night from St Daniel's hill."

I simply nodded; I needed Joan's cooperation to nip this blight on our town in the bud.

"You're absolutely right Joan if we were talking about a few scraps of paper that the bin-boys had dropped, but this is a wholesale mess. All the way up the Lower Lamphey road was strewn with rubbish, ashes in newspapers, empty food tins, cereal packets and leftovers, not the work of foxes I'd say, considering that all the bins were upright and still half full."

Joan acceded. "Truth be told, it's never been more than a few bins turned over by the town's naughty boys. I'll find out what my husband has got to say about it all and will report back when we meet in Brown's café during the week."

I was about to close my needlework box to confirm that the most important part of our gathering was complete when Beryl the Will piped up. She didn't speak often. She was married to the town clerk, a solicitor who it seemed had trained her in the art of saying less to achieve more. She said he had constantly reminded her that the fewer words he had included in any will he had drawn up, had usually ensured that a family row didn't take place. Well, at least not at the reading.

"What happened to the pieces of paper that weren't wrapped around ashes?" Beryl's accent still linked her to her Swansea beginnings, even though she and her husband had moved west to take

2

up their rural practice some seventeen years ago.

"Good point Beryl!" agreed Joan the Tip. "I'll add that into my little chat with my husband tonight."

It was plain to me that our work was done at this meeting, I locked up after everyone had left and went home, up the side of the Wesleyan church towards the Police station.

***

Brown's café was packed. It was the favourite haunt of shoppers who staggered in having stripped the shelves of the Melias grocery shop opposite, emptied Smith the butcher's window and claimed their full family allowance from the post office next door. The latter was requested in small coinage mind you, most of them lived in a pay through the meter world. I had invited Beryl to join me and Joan to examine the mounting mystery of the wayward rubbish at the Station Road end of town.

Beryl had the shortest distance to travel to the café. She and her husband lived nearby in one of the bigger terraced houses on the Chained Back as it was known. A spiked chain ran along the edge of their elevated road to afford the visitors and tradesmen protection from the drop on to the Main Street. Barry the Post told everyone he was not convinced; he was often quoted to have said that he had been injured more times by the chain than the bites he had received from the few deranged dogs on his round.

Beryl stepped in front of me. She was able to gain three places immediately by asking out loud, in her broadest Swansea accent,

"Has Sergeant Evan's wife arrived yet?"

The row of bench seats nearest the door were vacated at high speed. The more observant patrons amongst the customers might have noticed that the seats had been occupied by travelling salesmen and their accompanying over-zealous debt collectors who constantly plagued the more austere doorsteps in the town. Not to mention their preference to be seated near the door to escape any physical assaults which might accompany a formal complaint about the shoddy toys delivered at the Christmas just past. Unnecessary really, because most of the children knew that if a toy had 'Made in Hong Kong' stamped underneath it, then any car with more than one wheel remaining after an hour of robust play was indeed a bargain.

I waited until the waitress had cleared away the debris of chocolate wrappers, crisp packets and half-finished mugs of tea left on the table. When our order for three teas, in proper cups mind you and an ice-cream sundae with two additional saucers complete with spoons had been accurately relayed, I asked Joan to share her findings.

"My husband was spitting feathers all the way through his tea." She dabbed her lips gently with her paper napkin. I could only imagine the spectacle of a mouthful of feathers and a corned beef pie flashing before her!

Joan pressed on. "It was the third time in as many weeks that he and the dustbin boys had found a whole street in a shambles. They had to clear it all up as well as completing their round. They finished late but their tightwad of a manager refused to pay them overtime. He said that they must have been rushing the collection to get home before the rain had set in. My husband said that the reason that the Sergeant had seen the most recent mess was because the Lamphey road collection wasn't due until the afternoon. The others, a street at the top of the Green estate and another in Orange Gardens had been cleared up before the Sergeant had arrived."

I wanted a few answers. "Did you find out about any notepapers or letters being tipped out?"

Joan tilted her head. "I did get round to that but he told me that the funny thing was that they didn't find any paper of that kind in the bins or on the ground."

Beryl the Will looked worried. "I was afraid of that, this isn't young boys playing about. The culprits could be looking for details about each household, their private business you see. My husband insists on burning all our bills and out-of-date receipts on a bonfire in the garden."

Joan swallowed a large spoonful of vanilla ice-cream giving herself a short brain freeze. She blinked furiously and shuddered. Her voice croaked. "Not everyone in Pembroke has the luxury of a garden but why would the bin raiders only take the paper with them?" She swallowed, then added in her normal voice. "Not that I would complain if they took the back page of the Western Telegraph which

4

delights in reporting the lower position of the Pembroke rugby team in the second division. Gives my husband a headache it does."

I'd heard enough. I turned to Beryl. "Sergeant Evans." I paused as is my way, I liked to award my husband his full rank regularly, "carried out a few enquiries at my suggestion at the houses near to the scene of the alleged crime, even though he said that he hadn't sent many people up to Swansea prison for stealing rubbish!" I ran my spoon around the glass sundae dish to capture the last of the raspberry sauce and licked the spoon clean taking my time.

"It seems that the paper items in the bins weren't stolen after all. Most of the householders found them stuffed in the hedges or behind their front garden walls."

Joan looked relieved. "That explains why the Bin boys couldn't find any. Now it's no longer a crime scene, as they say on the Dick Barton radio serial, it looks like it's the naughty boys again."

Beryl the Will liked to flick her naturally blonde hair from her shoulders,

"I'm still not convinced that it's children. If they go out any evening to cause trouble, it's usually in their own backyard so to speak. Not to mention that most houses put their bin out last thing at night. This is a deliberate pattern moving up through the town. Wouldn't surprise me if they do come back. I bet if they do, they'll follow the same pattern. Most likely the next rubbish raid will be on another street on the Green estate."

I was thinking as I carefully stacked the empty cups and saucers into the middle of the table, upholding my firm belief that any place I visited had to be left tidier than I had found it. Standards you know. I took Beryl's proposal further, by asking Joan. "Which streets did they attack on the Green estate and in Orange Gardens?"

"Thought you might ask me that, my husband said it was Woodbine Terrace and South Street."

I flicked an imaginary crumb from my pleated skirt. "It's making a bit of sense now. They are, if I'm not mistaken, the longest roads in that part of the town. Our litter vandals wouldn't be able to pick out the paper in the dark so they are intending to empty as many bins as they can in the short time between first light and when the dustbin lorry arrives."

5

Joan held her forehead. "Taking this all in then", she paused as she thought things through. "If they do go back to the Green estate next week, it's likely that the next longest street being St Anne's Crescent will be on their list. Considering the length of the bin raiders working day, we'd need to be up early to catch them red-handed."

Beryl came back into the deliberation. "Florrie the Fire, one of our members you know who has openly admitted that she has a thing about the Fire Station Chief, even though he's a confirmed bachelor and all, recently did a house exchange over to the Green estate to be nearer to her family. She might know someone in St Anne's Crescent who could keep watch for us."

I wasn't too happy letting our mission rest on the fortunes of Florrie's romantic pursuits. Everyone knew that the real reason she moved over to the Green estate was to be close to the home of her long-time heart's desire. It had been reported within the Sewing Circle that on his last two call-outs the hapless fireman had been followed all the way to Pembroke Dock fire station by a well-wrapped up and mysterious figure on her Rudge bicycle.

I picked up my handbag so that my friends would know that this sub-meeting of the Station Road Sewing Circle was coming to a close. "Best if we pick up the trail with Florrie then, at our full Circle meeting next week," I announced. "Time is running out in our quest to keep the streets of our town clean and tidy."

***

I have to be fair, the members of the sewing circle paid full attention to Myvvi the Dead's demonstration of applique embroidery. Even her choice of a shroud as the garment to be decorated didn't divert them from their attempts to follow her basic instructions. She deftly showed them how to emblazon a large red dragon where the wearer's national identity would be proudly displayed. The round of applause given by her sister members kindly glossed over the fact that most of Myfanwy's husband's late departed clients would have come from the Pembroke surroundings. Him being the town undertaker and all, his patron's national origins would never have been in doubt. But as Carol from Chapel pointed out, Saint Peter at his pearly gates might not have the details of every person's home country printed on his selective list of those to be given a clear entry to paradise.

I was on my feet before Myvvi had packed away the last of her garments best suited for travelling to the afterlife. I outlined the progress made on solving the mystery of why the town was being subjected to the litter attacks.

I explained. "We, the investigation team, are of the opinion that they will strike again probably over in the Green estate. I would invite Florrie as a now established resident of that part of town, family ties are important as you all know." I paused to allow my observation to initiate the flicker of eyelids accompanied by soft coughs around the circle, "to join Joan, Beryl and me after this meeting has closed."

The remaining nine members of the circle understood to a girl, the urgency of the matter in hand. They rose, put their chairs up against the wall and had reached the door before I had put my hands on the lid of my sewing box, the official symbol of meeting closure.

Florrie couldn't wait. "I now live in Green Meadow Avenue but my mother and father have lived in St Anne's Crescent for years, she'll be more than happy to keep watch.

I wanted to be clear. "All we want to know is who is doing this, then we can find out why ruining our chances with the Welcome to West Wales judges is so important to them."

Joan chipped in. "Best in my book would be if they didn't know we were on to them. Remember when we used to go door knocking as girls?"

Florrie giggled. "They never saw the thread we had tied to the knocker because it was flat against the opened door."

Joan picked up the point. "Such fun and all the better that we annoyed the neighbours who had been nasty to us! Let's tie a thread between the dustbin lid and your mother's door knocker, muffled of course. As they lift the lid to find the paper they'll raise the alarm, your mother could look out of an upstairs' window to see them and they will be none the wiser."

Beryl asked. "Could I suggest one more addition to your excellent plan?"

She put her hand on Florrie's arm. "I wonder if you could pop over to your Mum's during the evening and make a list of the papers

7

she is throwing out, I still can't see the sense of pulling paper out from the bins and leaving it behind the wall."

The four detectives couldn't wait for Bin-day to arrive.

**

Our twelve faces sat around the tables in St Michael's church hall could be described as downright sad all the way up to highly annoyed. I had just announced that my reliable sources, mainly mothers taking the younger children to school, had confirmed that the rubbish collection at St Anne's Crescent had gone smoothly. There hadn't been a single scrap of evidence to be seen outside of the bins or indeed the dustbin lorry. Our paper trail, so to speak, had come to an abrupt end.

Beryl, I could sense, was intent on waiting for answers, she suggested. "I say we give it another week and stick to our plan. We have a few months to when the Welcome to West Wales judges might come. It's best we only make our next move with the full story in front of us."

Joan, who plainly supported her friend's conspiracy theory said. "I agree with Beryl, if they are coming back, it'll be in the Green Estate, we will just have to cast our net further, instead of our stitches so to speak, and wait." Her attempt to raise spirits gained little response.

I was about to invite Carol from Chapel to start her talk on the role of crochet work in holy decorations when the door crashed open and a red-headed whirlwind rushed in the door waving a piece of paper vigorously at all sitting around the table. They watched with open mouths as Florrie the Fire came over to me and dropped the piece of paper on to the table.

"Sorry for getting here late," she gasped. "there was a call-out to a bungalow on the Cosheston road, false alarm really – her chip pan had gone up in smoke, they never even got the chance to roll out their hoses!" She paused, realising that her whole purpose in life had been poured out in front of the entire gathering.

I had looked at the evidence in front of me. "Florrie, calm down girl, we understand why you're a bit excited but what has a list with a circle around the entry – 'Paid bill from Mrs Hayes corner shop' got to do with anything?"

Florrie sat down in her usual seat and having gained back some of her breath, continued. "As we had agreed, I went over to my mother's place in St Anne's Crescent, wrote a list of all the paper in her dustbin, put it out and tied the thread from the front door knocker to the bin lid. When I got home, I was about to put my own dustbin out when I thought it wouldn't be a bad idea to set up my own trap as I remembered that the bin lorry came around to my street - Green Meadow Avenue as they worked their way down the estate. Now there's good news and bad, the litterers indeed came to my road this morning, the knocker woke me up and I rushed to the bedroom window." She paused, as is the custom when delivering astounding news. "I saw the McCarthy twins rifling my bin, I should have said that my house is the first in the street. The not so good news is that as they were about to move on up the street one of them glanced up and saw me at the window, they ran off."

The entire room was enthralled.

Carol from Chapel said. "Well done girl, those twin boys are responsible for most of the petty theft in the town. They're at it again."

Joan the Tip was still intent on cheering us up. "What a sight girl! Seeing you in your bright red nightie at the window, that would've scared anyone off!"

Everyone laughed but I quickly brought things back to the matter in hand,

"That is simply brilliant Florrie, well done girl! You haven't finished yet have you?" I picked up the list, and jabbed the circled entry. Florrie grinned broadly. "They shuffled through my papers and one of them stuffed something in their pocket. However as expected, they put the rest behind my front wall. When I checked my list indoors, the only thing they took with them was my weekly bill from Hayes' shop."

Everyone present knew that the corner shops around town allowed credit through the week on the mutual understanding that all bills were settled on pay-day. Customers never for a moment thought about checking the listed purchases and shop-owners never felt the need to charge interest due to the loyalty afforded them by their captive customers.

I summarised. "We now know who has been emptying our bins but we don't know the why? Best if I mention to the Sergeant at tea that one of us saw the twins lurking around the bins in Green Meadow Avenue. Perhaps a doorstep chat with their mother Cynthia might bring this matter to a close. We can then start to enjoy our sewing and knitting and look forward to greeting the Welcome to West Wales judges whenever they turn up."

Beryl didn't seem to be so sure. "Cynthia bless her, is a widow. My husband the solicitor, had to help her with a few county court orders barely a month before the late Mr McCarthy fell overboard from the Kathleen and May schooner tied up at the town quay. The coroner decided that it was an accidental death and not related to the official lock-in which had just finished in the adjacent public house. She has no control over her boys who I think are more unruly than bad. All their antics have been aimed at getting some money into her purse. I'd like to know the real reason they had for taking paid bills out of the dustbins."

I nodded. "I agree that we shouldn't put Cynthia through any more than she's got on her plate, I'll suggest that my husband invites the boys to a friendly chat at the station. It'll be interesting to see what comes out after they've spent five minutes in a cell."

***

Joan, Beryl and Florrie were sat back, bathing in their anticipated glory for bringing the mystery of the rifled dustbins to an end.

I called the meeting to order. "We have a very satisfactory outcome to share with you and can say with confidence that Pembroke town will once again be tidy as well as welcoming."

The stillness in the church hall amplified my explanation,

"Following my gentle suggestion, Police Sergeant Evans conducted a paternal chat, in the absence of their late father, with the McCarthy twins. Their motive it seems was to raise money to give to their mother. A nice man had approached them when they were coming up the Gooses Lane from the park who said that if they could collect a handful of paid bills from the dustbins for him, they would

10

be paid threepence each time. He even told them which streets to visit and when. He also explained that relieving binmen of their rubbish before they took it to the tip was not as far as he knew a crime."

Beryl was wanting more of our answers to be made public. "Tell us then, who was the nice man and why was he happy to pay good money for shopping bills that had been already paid mind you?" Her broad Swansea accent added urgency to her request.

"I was coming to that! Sergeant Evans is a compassionate officer of the law who persuaded the boys to tell him all about their benefactor. So, it was in the lounge bar of the Lion Hotel that he caught up with the nice man responsible for the twin's misdemeanours."

I was starting to sound like I'd had memorised the last few entries in my husband's note-book. "Through decisive questioning he was able to discern that the man before him was the South Wales sales manager for a company which was conducting a promotion of ex-war department furniture at rock bottom prices. The bargains were only to be made available to deserving customers in Pembroke and the surrounding villages. He said that by analysing the binned bills and knowing what people could afford to eat, his salesmen would only knock-on needy doors. He must have thought that my husband had just arrived in town on one of the six trains a day that come down from Carmarthen."

From previous such announcements, the entire sewing circle knew that I had added that in to build up my final revelation.

"The sales manager insisted that he only used the bills for market research and that he destroyed them later. My husband pointed out that selling goods to people who can barely pay their way could well destroy the family. It was then that the manager gave his game away, he said that hire purchase was the way of the future and that by stretching out the payments for a modest interest people could afford things they had only dreamed of.

As sharp as one of his notebook's pencils, the Sergeant replied 'so that's where you make your money, they end up paying much more in the long run. I'll tell you now, you won't be making another farthing out of the people of Pembroke or you'll be on a charge of aiding and abetting the pilfering of property belonging to the

Municipal tip'. The fellow didn't even finish his whisky and peppermint, he went straight upstairs and packed."

I sat down to gentle applause from the Circle, allowing a slight smile on my lips to convey that I didn't mind that the credit for solving this case would go entirely to my husband. I was more than happy to take any lesser morsel of praise for returning the town once again to being a worthy candidate for our fourth Welcome to West Wales award.

Caring for Cats – *Bron the Books*

I'm not very comfortable standing up in front of people. I much prefer the company of a good book, any book really. Just as well that I say it to myself as I'm the only librarian in Pembroke town. That said, the letter I had received on Saturday morning had to be read out to the entire membership of the Station Road Sewing Circle whether I was comfy about it or not.

Bessie the Law brought our Knitting for Korea session to a close, having announced that between us we had sent off twenty-two jumpers and fourteen vests to the needy children in Asia whose country had still not recovered from their war.

"Now then Bron, over to you, I believe you have news for us from within the hallowed halls of our library!"

I stood up and pulled out the letter which had robbed me of a great deal of sleep all over the weekend. "I received this," I waved the wafer-thin grey paper in front of me, "from a very good customer of the library, namely Miss Hyacinth over in Markson Hall. She has asked me to pop out to feed her two cats while her housekeeper and the gardener, a married couple are away on their annual family visits. She says that whilst her sister Miss Holly is very ill in the West Wales General Hospital in Carmarthen, due to her own circumstances she herself is unable to look after Ruby and Emerald. Two things I must say, she thinks the world of her two pets, gems they are to her and as I have never owned a cat, I wouldn't know the first thing about seeing to their needs."

Bessie interjected. "Bron love, no need to be worried on that account, plenty of us here have cats and a show of hands would tell you who would be more than pleased to help you out."

I shook my head. "Thank you for that, I probably would have

found the answers in a book on one of the library shelves, it's more of a concern to me where she sent me this letter from." I waved the notepaper again. "The heading on this is 'Pembrokeshire Police – Haverfordwest Castle - Remand Wing'."

Joan the Tip gasped. "What on earth is she doing in there?"

I said. "They are going to charge her with poisoning her sister Holly."

At least eight hands, all belonging to well-experienced cat owners shot up into the air, a sewing circle mystery had surely beckoned.

***

I was so relieved that Maggie the Shop and Myvvi the Dead had volunteered to help me with my mission to look after the cats. I opened up a new bottle of Bulmer's full-strength cider the moment the three of us entered my flat above the library.

Maggie gave her approval. "We need something a bit stronger than tea if we are going to get that poor woman out of prison. I might only know her from every Thursday when her gardener drives her into town to do a bit of shopping but I tell you this, she is very much a lady. She wouldn't harm anybody, least of all her own flesh and blood."

I agreed with her. "Miss Hyacinth and Miss Holly had always lived with their late aunt but it was Miss Hyacinth who enjoyed the gentler side of country living. She has always been a bit fussy though, she liked reading but wouldn't have any library books which had been previously handled, so to speak, by anyone else. I arranged to send her a list of all the new releases each month so that she could make a selection which I would then send out to the Hall as soon as they came in.

Myvvi piped up. "To keep a balanced eye on all of this it's worth saying, the sisters didn't get on all that well. My husband and I buried their aunt out at Cresselly eighteen months ago. There was something in her bequest about at least one of the girls having to live at Markson Hall for as long as the cats were alive. Beryl the Will told me it was a difficult reading for her husband their family solicitor. Miss Holly, was more of a city girl and had recently returned from Bristol. She

14

can't wait to get back there. She simply wants to sell up and get back to her busy life in England.

I confirmed. "Miss Hyacinth on the other hand worships the two tortoiseshell brindles, Ruby and Emerald, she calls them her naughty torties."

Maggie brought us back to the truth of it all. "Can we agree that this could have the makings of a miscarriage of justice? We must find out how Miss Holly ended up in hospital and why the police are convinced that Miss Hyacinth put her there. I think a trip out to Markson Hall to feed our new feline friends is called for. We've stocked the shop with the new Whiskas brand of cat-food, they won't turn their noses up at a few tins of that, I'm sure."

Myvvi added. "My Hillman Minx hasn't been used to carry mourners for weeks now, staying in the garage – spotless it is, it's ready for a good run out this evening. There will be enough times over the next few weeks for Bron here having to cycle out."

We went with Maggie up to her shop, picked up the cat food then strolled down to the Undertakers premises on the Town Quay. Myvvi drove her car out of the garage. She was right to say it was sparkling, it proved to be comfortable too.

***

It was still quite bright when we drove up the short lane and parked on a wide gravel area alongside an Armstrong Siddely Sapphire. Its immaculate appearance would have given Myvvi's gleaming Hillman Minx a run for its money. Markson Hall couldn't be described as a stately home but it would by most, be safely considered to be a well-kept manor house. I retrieved the back door key from inside the greenhouse as directed by Miss Hyacinth's letter and we stepped into a large modern kitchen complete with the mandatory AGA cooker. I had read that they were bringing in new colours to replace the standard cream model, this one was a gentle pastel blue. Miss Hyacinth had said that she enjoyed cooking, no doubt this room was her domain. On the worktable was a recipe book surrounded by ingredients. I looked at the open page to see that a Cottage pie had been on the menu.

15

Maggie leaned over. "That must have been last Thursday's meal. Miss Hyacinth didn't come into the shop and no doubt didn't go into the butcher's two doors down for her Welsh beef mince."

Myvvi added. "Her sister must have been admitted to hospital overnight and Hyacinth was arrested before she could even dip her hands into the flour."

I shivered to think that if any poison was going to be administered, it would have probably taken place in this very room.

Maggie led us into a large dining room, she called out. "I've found the little lodgers, they're up on the top of the sideboard."

I went in to see a pair of furry faces looking down from the top of an antique Welsh dresser. They didn't seem to be upset at all by our intrusion. They only stirred when Maggie returned to the kitchen, found a tin-opener and the pungent but not unpleasant aroma of Whiskas filled the air. It was clear that Maggie had formed a friendship for life as the tortoiseshell pair rushed into the kitchen and tucked into the generous helping in their bowls.

We found Myvvi in the living room. She was thumbing through the books she had seen on the long polished side table. "Your Miss Hyacinth had a wide taste in books it seems." She turned to me. "there's everything here from romance to social history. She didn't believe in buying new though, all of these are library books with a single stamp inside the cover showing that she was the first borrower."

"For all her fussy and old-fashioned values," I explained as we wandered about trying to have a good look without touching anything else. "She tried to keep up with things. I'm already keeping an eye out for the second James Bond adventure, it's due out in a couple of weeks."

My eyes took me across the heavily laden shelves in a solid oak open bookcase. It was populated with the usual sets of limited editions and encyclopaedias. The evening sun glinted back at me from a book on the top shelf almost out of reach. I realised that it had been given a protective plastic covering much like I would put on the new more expensive books when they first arrived at the library. I was thankful that the most fitting description of me during my school days was 'tall and gangly beyond her years'. I reached up on my toes and pulled the book out. It was entitled 'At last, a Weed-Free Garden.' I opened it and wished I hadn't.

"This is a library book with a card inside made out to a Miss H Markson. I remember this book coming in a few months ago but I've never sent it out here."

Maggie looked at me. "Are you sure, it could have slipped your mind!"

I sighed. "The card is from Tenby library, this was ordered behind my back so to speak."

Myvvi spoke in the voice she usually reserved for grieving relatives. "I know it's upsetting when you find out something about someone who you have a high level of respect for. What's a gardening book going to tell us about Miss Hyacinth's predicament?"

I had turned over to the contents page. "It's becoming worse - there's a chapter underlined here called – Sodium Chlorate how to prevent harm to humans and pets."

Maggie whistled. "That's the last thing we wanted to find on her bookshelf. The more we find out here the less we seem to know about this lady."

Myvvi said. "I know I've been doubting Hyacinth up to now but we need to know what the poor girl is going through. Do you think they'll be allowing her visitors? We ought to go see them both. I had some dealings with Holly over her aunt's funeral, she can be a bit of a madam. Me and Bron could go to the West Wales hospital to pay her a friendly but of course, concerned visit."

Maggie caught her drift. "Then Bron and me could go over to the Remand Centre in Haverfordwest to let Hyacinth know how we are getting on with her cats."

I agreed with them but I wanted to see Hyacinth first. "Let's go to see the real victim in all of this before we do anything else!"

***

The policemen had shown Maggie and me into a brightly lit room, bare but for a table with chairs each side. There was a single chair by the door. He told us where to sit and we waited for Hyacinth to arrive.

I was half expecting her to be dressed in a uniform with broad

17

arrows running up it but she had a skirt and plain top on, worn but still tidy. Her face lit up when she saw us but the large smudges under her eyes confirmed to me that the Remand Centre sleeping arrangements were nothing like indeed her own bed.

The policeman sat by the door.

Maggie confirmed that the torties were well and that they had taken to the latest cat-food with evident vigour. She added quickly that the new diet had probably taken their appetite and attention away from their mistress being absent.

I asked Hyacinth. "What's the food like in here?"

She mouthed 'awful' before confirming "It isn't all that bad."

Maggie lowered her voice. "What evidence have they produced against you?"

Hyacinth shrugged. "Apparently Holly has been given small amounts of a gardening chemical, over a few weeks or so." Her voice broke but she recovered. "If she'd had it all at once it could have killed her."

I asked. "Are they saying because you do the cooking, that's how you gave it to her?"

"We only eat together in the evenings so the only food she doesn't prepare for herself is that meal. I can't believe that this is all happening. She's a real pain to me over Ruby and Emerald but she is my sister. I wouldn't even know how to do such a thing. We leave all the garden business to O'Brien our gardener."

I persisted. "Tell us about your evening meal routine so that we can understand where the police are coming from."

"I simply cook the evening meal and plate it up. Holly doesn't like eating it when it's hot, so I put the meals on the food trolley to cool off. I then nip upstairs to change for dinner. When I come down, I take them into the dining room. Holly is usually sat up at the table waiting."

Maggie wanted to know. "You both have the same meal don't you, you could pick up either plate, how would you know which plate was intended for your sister?"

Hyacinth blushed. "I don't like eating my greens but Holly can't have enough of them. Her plate is always piled high."

For the first time my faith in this all being an injustice wobbled. I sighed. "So as you plate up every night you would know exactly which meal would end up in front of your sister?"

"That's what the police are saying. They insist that I have plenty of time to put something in her food."

I needed to dig down, our visit was confirming her guilt, not giving her back her freedom. "The only other time the food could be tampered with is when you were upstairs changing, is there anyone you can think of who would need to go into the kitchen at that time?"

Hyacinth welled up. "Ruby and Emerald are allowed in the kitchen to eat their food, but this is not their doing. I don't want to give my sister any reason at all to get rid of them. She's only interested in selling our home."

Maggie knows about cats, she has two that live in and a couple of strays who hang around the back of her shop for scraps. "How can you be sure that your torties haven't picked up any chemicals in the garden and brought them in with their paws? If I'm not wrong, your Ruby with her huge appetite would be very likely to take an interest in your food whether it was hot or cold."

Hyacinth dabbed under her eyes and said carefully. "I take every precaution to ensure that there has been no contact between Ruby and my sister's plate."

I'd had enough. "You need to be honest with us Hyacinth love, is there a connection between Ruby and this entire business. You can't sacrifice years of your life for a cat surely?"

Hyacinth put her hands on the table and looked at us both in turn. "Over the past few months, I've been finding Ruby sat on the table next to the food trolley, not every night mind you. The table is on the same side where I put Holly's plate. I have been switching them over and giving Holly my meal to make sure that a single cat's hair can't find its way on to her plate."

"Just a minute," Maggie stopped herself from raising her voice and alerting the policeman by the door. "You said she has plenty of greens, you don't have time to do it all over do you?"

Hyacinth gave us a faint smile. "I simply move her greens on to what was my plate."

I had another question which had been burning my tongue off. "Have you ever used another library other than mine?"

19

Her eyes, still damp widened. "Of course not, you have given me all the reading I could ever want."

The policeman stood up and announced that our time was up.

I placed my hands over Hyacinth's. "Try not to worry, whatever you've told us today will go no further. This has been a very useful visit. We'll be doing all we can to get you back to Markson Hall before you know it."

***

Maggie and me made good use of the bus-ride from Haverfordwest down to Neyland. We went over every detail we could draw out from our chat with Hyacinth. Before I knew it, we were off the bus and walking down to the ferry.

"From what we've learned," she summarised. "it appears that Hyacinth who is the supposed poisoner is in fact the poisonee, so to speak. in that, she has been giving, from time to time, her poisoned platter to her sister."

"We can't rule out Ruby the wayward cat, she could be contaminating her plate, she's near enough when she jumps up on to the table."

"Then again," Maggie cautioned me. "There may be another way that the chemical is arriving in the kitchen, come to think of it we could try to find it in the greenhouse or the small potting shed next to it."

I wanted to unravel things further. "We could walk up to the Hall from the other side of the ferry to feed the cats, there'll be enough light to have a rummage in the outbuildings."

There were still quite a few loose threads in all of this but I was feeling that some of it was coming together in one picture, you might say a bit of a tapestry.

We alighted at Hobbs Point to find Myvvi waiting in her Hillman Minx. A welcome sight indeed!

"I couldn't wait to hear how your trip has gone," she explained. "I thought you could do with a lift up to the Hall."

We sped along the London Road and in no time at all were going up the lane to Markson Hall.

"That's interesting," remarked Maggie. "There's smoke coming out of the gardener's cottage chimney. I thought the O'Brien's were still on their travels."

"They might have been contacted by the police," I suggested. "It wouldn't do any harm for us to explain what we're doing here."

Myvvi smiled. "You mean the apparent reason – feeding the kitties."

An older man with an outdoor face on him emerged from the cottage. He was wearing dungarees which had seen better days. I explained that we were there by Hyacinth's invitation.

He shook his head. "A nasty business in any family, rest assured my wife and I will be keeping well out of it all. She will be more than happy to feed the cats though, now we are back."

I decided that a simple question would save us the bother of finding an excuse to nose around the place. "You keep a lovely garden; you must spend dawn to dusk keeping the weeds down?"

His face beamed. "They don't get a look in here, careful mulching and being quick with the hoe sends them on their way. I follow my father you know, a natural approach to husbandry is vital."

I gathered that he didn't have many opportunities to share his horticultural wisdoms.

"Another thing I'll tell you for free, you won't find a single bug on my roses," he paused to see if we were following him, our half open mouths were good enough. "I plant mint between the rose bushes, aphids and the like can't stick the smell of it."

We were saved from the next instalment of his well-thumbed gardening hints by Mrs O'Brien coming out of the cottage door, she looked every inch a housekeeper, there wasn't a scrap of clothing on her that hadn't been well starched. "What's going on here then," she was smiling. "I sent him over to the post box to collect our letters and here he is chatting up three young ladies."

I explained our presence to which she responded. "Well thank you for looking after Ruby and Emerald, lovely torties those two. Terrible business up at the Hall, coming on top of all she was having to put up with."

Maggie wanted the same answer as me, but I couldn't think how best to ask it, she said. "It's not very nice being cooped up in there all

21

day is it?"

Mrs O'Brien responded with "Miss Holly might have a private ward, but hospital food is the same the world over. She'll be missing her sister's cooking."

I realised that the O'Brien's had only been given half the story, however I was intrigued with anything that Holly was having to put up with. "She was suffering a bit before all this business then?" I tried to be as sympathetic as I could."

Mrs O'Brien obliged me. "Nonstop it was, sometimes several letters a week. I take the mail up each morning to the living room from the box at the bottom of the lane you see. Whilst I would never look at private correspondence, the address of the debt collection company was plain enough on the back of the envelope. They are the only letters we have ever had from Bristol, must be to do when she lived up there."

I was pleased with the O'Brien's voluntary information but I needed to pay one last visit to the Hall.

"Could we feed the cats one final time," I asked. "We can say our goodbyes and all then."

Mrs O'Brien gave us her approval and then pointed to the lane to remind her husband that he was in the middle of his errand.

Ruby and Emerald didn't seem all that bothered about our efforts to give them a fond farewell. I went into the living room and collected the now overdue library book.

***

Myvvi and me sorted out our plan of action as we sped along the Carmarthen Road up to the hospital. My earlier phone call had confirmed that Miss Holly had been moved into a private room prior to her imminent discharge. We duly entered through the paying patients' entrance and were shown by a nurse to the room in question. The décor was as good as any room you'd find in the Lion Hotel back in Pembroke. Soft drapes, deep carpets and more pastel shades than you'd find on a decorator's paint chart. Sat in a comfortable armchair looking as well as anyone royal was Holly in her brocade dressing gown.

We were barely in the door when she greeted Myvvi, ignoring me. "It's good of you to visit but if you'd waited a few more days, I'd be able to welcome you into Markson Hall."

Myvvi introduced me as a friend of Hyacinth's and opened up our rehearsed response. "We wanted to see that you had recovered fully from your ordeal and to let you know that the cats are in the pink of health."

She retorted. "A bit pointless don't you think coming thirty miles to give me bad news."

Myvvi smiled grimly. "Well there are a few things that we'd like to clear up with you, bearing in mind that your sister is still in custody."

"Nothing to do with me," she scoffed. "If the Pembrokeshire police want to trump up charges against an innocent person, that's down to them."

I piped up. "You don't think your sister had anything to do with your illness then?

"Of course not, she's too soft and doesn't have the backbone to harm a fly."

Myvvi nipped in. "How do you think the poison found its way into your body?"

"No idea. Must have picked it up somewhere. I've had a lot on my mind lately, not to mention my sister who puts those horrible animals before me and my well-being."

"You don't like living there with them, do you? Myvvi pressed her. "You'd rather sell up and go back to your city life in Bristol?"

"City life for sure instead of a backwater like Pembroke, not sure if it would be Bristol though."

"Too many debts to settle I dare say," Myvvi ventured. "We saw the letters piling up back at Markson Hall."

Holly looked at her silk slippers. "That's a private matter which is none of your business."

I came in on cue. "I can tell you what isn't a private matter," I reached into my bag and pulled out a plastic-covered book entitled 'At last, a Weed-Free Garden.', this library book is public property, and to boot, it is now overdue." I opened the cover and showed the contents page to Holly. "You needn't worry about being called to account for defacing the book, I've rubbed out the pencil marks on a

23

certain chapter which no doubt you've had a personal interest in."

Her face was red, she spoke in a whisper. "You appear to have worked out what's been going on. Perhaps you'd like to tell me how the poison arrived on the wrong plate."

That's the nearest we'll ever get to a confession I thought.

Myvvi stepped in. "What we know about your goings-on isn't the important thing here. We have a proposal which we don't think you're in a position to refuse."

Holly slumped in the chair. "Let's get this over with!"

***

The Station Road Sewing Circle was more than ready to hear how Maggie, Myvvi and me had restored peace and goodwill at Markson Hall. Maggie explained how we had convinced both sisters to a sworn secrecy for their own benefit but most of all to keep our involvement out of it.

"We agreed between us that Holly would never know that her younger sister had been unwittingly putting the poisoned meals in front of her and Hyacinth would never find out that her sister had planned for her to be so ill that control of the Hall's finances would be taken away from her. Holly agreed to contact the police in Haverfordwest to explain that she had somehow picked up the poison and to request her sister's release.

Myvvi then said. "They both were in receipt of a generous allowance from their aunt's estate. Due to her lavish lifestyle, Holly had run up considerable debts in Bristol. Hyacinth on the other hand had quite a bit of savings because she had led a quiet life looking after her aunt. We persuaded Holly to take an interest-free loan from Hyacinth to pay off her debts. The loan would be repaid when eventually the Hall would be sold."

I summarised. "I agreed to send the library book back to Tenby and to explain that because of illness no fine should be paid. The main piece of literary evidence against Holly would soon be circulating around the gardeners of the seaside town. I also popped out to Markson Hall to collect the almost full bottle of weed-killer, which Holly had been keeping under lock and key in a box under her bed. I left it early one morning outside the Agricultural Merchants in Carew with a little note tied to it.

'*Please find attached bottle, the contents of which are no longer required. Long live Weeds.*' Before I had sat down three ladies were heading for the kitchen to put the kettle on. Tea with Bessie the Law's heavy bread pudding would go down nicely as we all chewed over the ins and outs of the now-solved mystery at Markson Hall.

Nowhere much to Sit - *Megan the Signals*

I was wedged in the box seat of Granny Gwyneth's front window, one hand holding my cup of tea and a huge slice of Bara Brith in the other.

I asked her. "Where exactly have your two Welsh stick armchairs gone to Gran? You've had them here in the front room for as long as I can remember."

I hoped that she didn't think I was complaining about having nowhere comfortable to sit.

"Longer than that Megan," her eyes twinkled. "My great grandfather made them, they couldn't afford to get their furniture from any shop, come to that not even a carpenter, if the man of the house couldn't make it, they sat on the floor."

I was more curious than worried,

"That makes them family heirlooms, more than likely over a hundred years old, what have you done with them?"

Granny Gwyn as we all called her settled back in her well-padded armchair, I could feel one of her stories starting to take shape. I wasn't wrong.

"It was last week when a Tenby girl got lost on her way to Cold Blow!"

I was now more worried than curious. "How did she manage that, she would have come through Cold Blow hamlet to get here from Tenby?"

Granny Gwyn chided me. "Hark at you, since your husband took the move from Templeton to Pembroke station have you become a suspicious townie? Your country upbringing would have told you that there's nothing awkward about helping a damsel in distress."

I polished off the last of the Bara Brith, a full mouth helps with the listening.

Granny Gwyn continued. "Vera had a large map flapping about in her hand, I couldn't see it very well so I asked her to come in to put it on the table. I pointed out that she needed to go back down the road for two miles. As she was folding up the map, she saw the stick chairs and said that they were beautiful. They are truly a part of Welsh culture; they would fetch a good price at any of the auctions conducted around the county. I wasn't all that keen to start with but she reminded me that prices only go up in the village shop and that at my age I'm entitled to a few extras."

I cleared the last of the succulent cake from my throat. "They are your chairs, Gran. Do with them as you wish. I was a bit worried that she might not be everything she seemed to be."

Granny Gwyn snorted. "I've been on God's earth for many more years than most but let me tell you Megan my girl that I'm nowhere near ready to go under it. I insisted that she give me a receipt for the chairs and she even gave me her full name and address. Not to mention that she asked me to sign a note which authorised them to sell the chairs on my behalf."

She went over to the sideboard, took out a business card and a piece of paper from the top drawer and thrust them into my still sticky hand. There it was in black and white, a perfectly straightforward business transaction with a second-hand furniture dealer from Tenby. I felt a such a fool.

"I'm sorry Gran if I doubted you, it's just that you read so much in the papers these days, so many people are preying on the older population."

Granny Gwyn laughed. "You're not the first to think I need a bit of looking after, you needn't worry girl, the next auction she told me is in the Pembroke branch of the auctioneers in a couple of days. This time next week I'll be sat here holding my money. Let the matter drop and I think it's time to show you my prize rhubarb crown in the garden from which my village-famous marmalade is made. I might even send you back to Pembroke with a pot of it in your basket."

That was the end of it, Granny Gwyn was never shy in telling anyone when they'd outstayed their welcome. I remembered as a child when she used to ask us to make sure the front door was closed -

from the outside. To this day I'm very aware if she has decided that a visit is about to come to a close.

***

Glenys the Coal had shown us the best way to hand finish a quilt with a heavy cotton binding using a double stitch. She had added that the quilt was then guaranteed to stay on any bed, regardless of how unsettled the occupant's night had been. We then moved into our refreshment groups inside St Michael's church hall to have tea and a bit of Myvvi the Dead's mountainous sponge cake. She was the first to point out that although her work as our town undertaker's wife mainly related to the lowering of the departed into the ground, she always took delight in making a sponge that rose well up in its tin.

I was sharing with Auntie Sian and Maria from Milan the events of yesterday when I'd gone up to visit my grandmother in Templeton.

"I made a right show of myself." I confessed. "She had to show me all the paperwork to shut me up. I still couldn't sleep a wink last night trying to piece together a girl who works for a furniture dealer who lives in Tenby taking a couple of chairs from Templeton to sell at an auction in Pembroke. All taking place out of a call on a random cottage to get directions? You'd think the young girl would have gone to a petrol station or indeed the village shop."

Auntie Sian nodded. "It's plain to me this has got you a bit worked up girl. Let's consider the good news first."

I was a bit sharp. "I know I can be a bit protective of my family but where's the good news in any of this?"

"You have said that they are to be auctioned here in Pembroke, if indeed there is any wrongdoing going on, it will take place within the Station Road Sewing Circle's boundary. That makes it an official investigation. We should let Bessie the Law know what we are up to before we head off down to the other end of town."

Auntie Sian was losing me. "What exactly are we doing and when?"

She smiled. "We'll find out the date and times of the auction, they'll be posted outside the town hall. We'll then get ourselves down to the saleroom to see the chairs for ourselves. Don't you love browsing through the lots before the auctioneer's hammer comes down."

Maria gave us her support. "Why don't you stay for the auction, you would know how much the chairs went for and if the same amount is passed on to your grandmother, you'll have nothing more to worry about."

My friends were right, the least we could do to help things along was to see that Granny Gwyn received a fair price for her family heirlooms.

***

We would have been mistaken if we had thought that going down in the morning to view the chairs that things would be quiet. The auction hall was teeming. Auntie Sian and I worked our way through the crowd towards the furniture section and after moving a couple of settees and sideboards we finally located Granny Gwyn's chairs. They had been tucked out of sight, almost as if the seller didn't want them to be noticed by too many would-be bidders. To be fair they looked old, not only the wear and tear inflicted upon them over the decades that the children in our family had climbed in and out of them but the original saw marks and chisel blisters left by my ancestor declared the feel of the rural artefact.

Auntie Sian suggested that we take a seat at the rear of the hall. The bidding was brisk as soon as the auctioneer mounted his platform. Porters skilfully replaced each item the moment they were sold to keep up the rapid pace at which most items, except the few which didn't reach their reserve price, gained a new owner. In next to no time I whispered to Auntie Sian. "Granny Gwyn's chairs are the next ones up, they should go for a pretty penny or two!"

The bidding started low and steadily climbed as several people in the room showed interest. I settled back to savour the sizeable funds which would keep Granny Gwyn comfortable for many a day. Suddenly the bidding ceased and a tall man in a green suit was lowering his numbered paddle. He had bought the chairs for a fraction of my estimation.

I almost shouted out. "There's been a mistake, those chairs are worth at least four times that amount." Instead, I whispered loudly into Auntie Sian's ear. "If there's any funny business going on in this hall, it's just taken place in front of our eyes."

Auntie Sian stood up. "Let's have another look at those chairs before they go out to be collected. The auction continued around us, paddles were being raised and lowered as if a giant puppeteer above had crossed his strings. We went around to the chairs which were now sporting bright yellow labels confirming that they had indeed been sold.

It was a bit too much, a sadness came over me as I stroked the battered arms and traced the bottom of the seat under which, as small children, we had played hide and seek. I was shaken out of my daydream when I felt a large rough label underneath. I gestured to Auntie Sian to help me turn the chair over. On a square of beaten leather, fastened by needle-thin panel pins were the words in a gothic gold; Three Counties Reproductions.

Auntie Sian confirmed our worst fears. "They've been sold as reproductions or modern copies, that's all your grandmother will get at best.

I spotted a well-dressed young lady coming through the side door, I grabbed Auntie Sian's arm pulling her to one side. "The girl who's just come in resembles the description Granny Gwyn gave me of that Vera, let's at least see where these chairs are going next.

We admired a large oil painting entitled 'Sunset over Freshwater East', I murmured to Auntie Sian. "I hope the new owners realise that the title refers to the place and not the direction in which to face to see it for themselves."

Over my shoulder, I saw Vera pick up one of the chairs and walk towards the entrance. I gestured for Auntie Sian to stay where she was as I followed Vera into the side street where she placed the chair in the back of a white van. A man climbed out of the driver's seat and held the door while she went back into the auction hall. The man was wearing a green suit.

***

I had invited Maria and Bessie to join Auntie Sian and me in Brown's café. Thursday morning included the weekly delivery of Eccles cakes. We ordered four with our tea as the owner proudly announced, 'You won't find a fresher cake outside of Yorkshire!' He is such a nice man that no one would ever suggest that he should brush up on his geography.

All teacups were half empty before Auntie Sian gave us the first of the reports,

"We know for a fact, that Granny Gwyn's genuine chairs had been labelled to look as if they were copies. Only the man in the green suit and his accomplice Vera could have done that. They knew that other bidders would drop out as soon as the chairs had reached their supposed value. Having legally bought the chairs at a knock-down price and removed the labels they are no doubt entering them in another auction somewhere in the county to make their money."

Bessie asked me. "Did you visit your Gran after the weekend?"

I nodded to confirm. "I don't think she really knew what they were worth, so I didn't tell her what had happened. Vera had popped over from Tenby and had given my Gran the proceeds, adding insult to injury mind you!

I paused and they waited, they knew that injuries would heal, unlike an insult which can leave a permanent scar.

"Vera said that as the chairs had been a family treasure her employer hadn't charged Granny Gwyn any commission."

You could have heard their short intakes of breath down the far end of the café.

Maria chipped in. "Can I give you my report now, I'm so excited that Bessie gave me my first mission on behalf of our Sewing Circle."

Bessie put her hand on Maria's arm. "Go ahead our Italian detective."

Maria said. "I checked through all the phone books in the Post Office and found a furniture maker and restorer in Maenclochog who trades as the Three Counties Reproductions. I rang him from the phone box and told him I was a well-to-do foreign resident making enquiries about his Welsh stick chairs. He said that the leather label I described to him was an old one, they had changed to paper labels to save on costs some time ago. He also said that his replica stick chairs could only be separated from the real thing by a proper expert. He has several stick chairs in stock and confirmed that the price is about the same as you would have to pay at auction for a reproduction."

She sat back looking very pleased.

"Well done girl," Bessie congratulated her, "that's very helpful. Unfortunately, we are too late to stop Granny Gwyn's chairs from disappearing over the horizon. We will have to come up with a way of turning the tables on Mr Green Suit and Vera or whatever she is calling herself today."

I gave Bessie a grim smile. "Don't you mean turning the chairs?"

She tapped the side of her head. "Sergeant Evans," she loved the sound of her husband's official title, "has many times said to me that criminals who think they have got away with it, always return to repeat the offence. We must take this pair on at their own game. I've been drawing up a bit of a plan but it will involve the use of a posh car, at least two more members of the Sewing Circle and believe it or not, the assistance of Granny Gwyn and one of her closest friends in Templeton."

Never mind fresh Eccles cakes I thought, you could cut the sizzle in the air with a knife.

***

Over the next few days, Bessie and I were so close you wouldn't be able to see the join. We asked Beryl the Will to have a few words with her husband, the Town Clerk about a small short-term loan from the Town's hardship fund. She explained to him that it was going to be used to help one of the Circle's family members who had received an income which was much lower than expected. He had no doubts on the matter when Beryl committed to it being paid back in full within the calendar month.

We asked Myvvi the Dead to use her immaculate Hillman Minx, more used to travelling respectfully behind her husband's hearse, to take Maria up to Maenclochog where she would purchase a pair of Welsh stick chairs. Auntie Sian was dispatched to confirm when the next auction was scheduled to take place in Pembroke.

My part in Bessie's increasingly complicated plot was to pay Granny Gwyn in Templeton another visit and without revealing what we were up to, gain her support along with her lifelong friend Granny Moll."

***

I was back in the window seat in the front room juggling yet another cup of tea and a plate of Welsh cakes balanced on the window sill. Granny Gwyn was surprised to see me but her reflexes had taken over as she made me welcome.

"Now then my girl," she started her interrogation. "I can see why you popped back earlier to see if Vera had given me my money but this visit is a bit too close for comfort?"

I had to respond. "How's Molly Jenkins getting on Gran? You and her have been friends more years than I've been around?"

Granny Gwyn smiled. "Typical you Megan, you always answer a question with another. As you've asked, Granny Moll is still drawing breath, at least she was yesterday when I saw her in the village shop. Now, are you going to tell me what this is all about?"

I put down my cup and held my hands up. "You've always been able to see through me. I have a friend, a foreign lady who has a pair of Welsh stick chairs that she needs to sell in a hurry. I thought that Granny Moll could help her."

Granny Gwyn was quick. "You want to sell them through Vera and allow her to think they are Granny Moll's family treasures, the dealer then won't charge commission giving all the proceeds to your foreign friend."

I couldn't have written the script better myself. I picked up another Welsh Cake. "What are you putting in these Gran, you're as sharp as a tack this morning?"

She brushed off an imaginary crumb from her long black skirt. "More than you think my girl, now let's get this bit of a lark underway. Who is going to let Vera know?" she rose and went over to the sideboard to bring out a business card. "Mollie and I are not too keen on the phone box up the lane, they say that Nosey Nellie down at the exchange listens in and that anything interesting is round the village the same day before she goes home for her tea."

I put my hand out for the card. "I'll catch a free ride, one of the

33

benefits of being a signalman's wife, from Pembroke station to Manorbier in a couple of days. Wouldn't be too clever if I called her from Pembroke. I'll tell her the truth that I'm your granddaughter and that you asked me to let her know you've heard of another pair of chairs in the village."

Granny Gwyn had that twinkle in her eye again. "I'll get myself down to Mollie's later today, she's out collecting gossip most mornings. She'll be more than happy to help this friend of yours out. She could put in a bit of drama for free, she only gave up being the fairy godmother in the village pantomime this last year. When can she expect the chairs?"

"They'll be here tomorrow, all going well, don't forget to tell Granny Moll that there'll be something in it for the pair of you if this all goes the way we expect it to."

Granny Gwyn giggled. "We'd welcome that indeed but having a bit of a goings on at our time of life is worth any bother."

***

The Station Road Sewing Circle was well represented at the auction in Pembroke. I had asked Bessie the Law if the six of us involved in the downfall of Mr Green Suit could be present when his comeuppance was delivered. Bessie agreed but only if everyone understood that the events could well get out of hand and that the consequences were too dreadful to think about.

Beryl and Myvvi arrived early and confirmed that true-to-form Granny Moll's chairs had been entered into the auction, delivered complete with fake leather labels, and had been placed out of sight away from any would-be bidders. They took their seats in the middle of the hall which was filling up nicely. Bessie preferred to stand at the back to watch her plot unfold. Auntie Sian and I took Maria to the registration desk and collected the numbered paddle which she would use to hurry things along. Maria sat near the aisle and Auntie Sian and I sat behind her.

As it turned out, the chairs had not been seen by anyone other than Beryl and Myvvi and of course Mr Green Suit. There were only two people present vying for the prize. As soon as Mr Green Suit had put in his first low bid, Maria's arm had shot up and raised her battle colours namely her numbered paddle. They soon reached the value of the apparent replica chairs. I caught sight of Mr Green Suit's smirk as he delivered his next bid which he hoped would cause Maria to drop out. All was going to plan. I started to feel nervous when Maria's arm went up barely a moment after her opponent's bid. His smirk had long gone as the bidding approached twice the value of the replica chairs. Bessie had assured us that because he was still aiming to make a sizeable profit it would be safe to bid further against him.

It was only when the bids had gone above three times what we had paid for the chairs that I knew things weren't going to plan. Mr Green Suit was wearing a furious expression indeed and had started to show his determination to get the chairs by bidding almost as quickly as Maria. Our Italian girl on the other hand looked as cool as a cucumber as she sent the bidding value soaring towards the real value of the chairs if they had been genuine.

If he stopped bidding and we had to pay for the chairs, Bessie had warned us that it would be legally binding, and the Sewing Circle would be in debt up to the end of the century.

I whispered harshly to Auntie Sian. "Did you tell Maria when to stop?"

Her face was ashen. "I did but I don't think she understood, she was more interested in waving the paddle about…"

I feverishly looked around. "At my signal get up as if you are leaving," I told her and pointed at a chipped and worn thirty-piece dinner service on a table in front of us. "Trip into that and send it flying."

Auntie Sian didn't hesitate when I put my hand on her shoulder, she stood up, took three steps and fell, taking the top six plates off with her elbow and the entire dinner service with her falling body. The enormous crash drew everyone's attention in the room, I leaned over Maria, wrestled the paddle out of her hand and with a sweep of my arm threw it out of the open window. The commotion died down after Auntie Sian had regained her feet and promised to pay for the damage. The auctioneer looked first at Mr Green Suit whose face was now bright purple, I think he had realised that his bout of auction fever to get the chairs at any cost had just removed any profit he thought he was going to make. The auctioneer reminded him that he had made the last bid. The bidding value that had been placed on the chairs was five times our purchase price. All eyes moved to Maria who stood and announced waving her empty hands "I am not able to bid anymore."

The auctioneer's hammer came down.

***

There wasn't a single knitting needle, crochet hook or reel of cotton in sight. The entire meeting of the Station Road Sewing Circle was devoted to the complete stitching up of Mr Green Suit. The several groups drinking their tea and working their way through Auntie Sian's Bara Brith Special, you could smell the Welsh whisky the minute you stepped in the door, were busy dissecting fact from fiction, or was it the other way around? Occasionally individual members moved into another group to give and to gain a different perspective on what actually happened in the auction room. I caught Bessie's eye as the group I was in had escalated Auntie Sian's involvement up to a smashed fifty-piece Royal Worcester, hand-painted dinner service worth a fortune. Bessie called our meeting to order and asked me to make the opening statement. I brought everyone up to speed by explaining the roles played by the two grannies in Templeton. It received spontaneous applause. Maria who appeared to have fully recovered from her dazzling performance at the auction explained how she and Myvvi had obtained the reproduction chairs from Maenclochog and delivered them to Granny Moll's house. She made us laugh when she explained that they couldn't get the Three Counties Reproductions paper labels off the bottom of the chairs. Granny Moll said that she hadn't worked as a postwoman for many years without knowing how to open the odd envelope or two. With the aid of a steaming kettle, the labels came off in one piece and the chairs looked every inch the genuine article.

Joan the Tip needed convincing. "What if Vera doesn't hand over the proceeds of the auction to Granny Moll, after all, it's Vera's employer's money?

Myvvi stood and put Joan's mind to rest. "We talked that over with Granny Moll, these old girls haven't come in on the last train from Whitland you know. Granny Moll said she would at first put up a bit of resistance but not enough to stop the deal going through. She said she would refuse to sign the printed note of authority but would be pleased to write and sign, in her best-printed lettering mind you, the note of authority to be handed to the auctioneer."

Myvvi smiled and waited, we all knew that the following sentence would seal it all.

"Granny Moll added a second paragraph unbeknown to Vera that the auctioneer should hold on to any proceeds which, would be collected in due course by her nominated representative. Everyone looked around the room to see who had played that particular part in this wide-ranging scheme. Beryl the Will stood up and patted her handbag,

"It's all here, divided into five shares. The first is going to pay off the loan from the Town's hardship fund. One share will go to Granny Moll for her Oscar-worthy performance and the three shares go to Granny Gwyn which will bring her proceeds up to the true value of her original chairs.

Our applause to all concerned rang out and took a while to subside.

Auntie Sian seemed to me to be a little pensive, Bessie spotted it too. "Out with it Auntie Sian, the auctioneer confirmed that the old dinner service you smashed wasn't worth much and so he wouldn't take a penny. We've also had a good victory over wrongdoing have we not?"

Auntie Sian lifted her hand. "Absolutely, I clapped as loud as anyone, but that crooked dealer will only lose a fraction on both deals when he sells those chairs. Not forgetting that he still has the profit in his pocket from Granny Gwyn's chairs."

Bessie looked at me. "Seeing that Megan the Signal's granny drew us all into this adventure, it's only fitting that Megan has the last word."

I coughed gently. "It is well known around the Pembroke area that a certain dealer who has a preference for green suits actually paid five times the going rate for a pair of fake chairs. It will only take a week for the village telegraphs to reach Tenby where he won't want to show his greedy face. Come to that, we won't be seeing him here in Pembroke for a good while. One final touch I need to share with you, which I believe will be to everyone's liking."

I paused to give the closure on the Welsh stick chairs caper it's due build-up.

"Following Auntie Sian's swan dive into the crockery, after I had given Maria's paddle its marching orders, I quietly went around to the collecting area and waited for the chairs. As soon as the porters had attached their yellow stickers and left, I removed the leather labels from under the seats and replaced the original Three Counties Reproductions version using a dollop of Granny Moll's homemade glue. She had assured me that it would take a blowtorch to get them off.

The most that our crook in the green suit will get for those reproduction chairs is what they are really worth."

I sat down.

Our roars of laughter accompanied by hoots of satisfied derision filled St Michael's church hall and spilled out through the open windows into Station Road. Passers-by could be forgiven I thought, for wondering how can such a celebration be going on from a group of women engaged in such a mundane activity as a sewing circle.

A Very Delayed Departure – *Myvvi the Dead*

Being the wife of the town undertaker, I took my half of the associated duties seriously to ensure that the demands for a quality send-off were well balanced against the value of the life insurance payout. Behind the closed doors of our chapel of rest, the division of responsibility was clearly set. My husband took very good care of the dead and I took charge of the living.

Despite the riveting examples from Megan the Signals, on how to maintain the tension of your wool when using four needles to knit a pair of socks, nothing could dislodge my graveside countenance.

I could see that Bessie the Law was conducting her weekly perusal of all present in the Station Road Sewing Circle, so it was no surprise to me when she singled me out and my close friend Carol from Chapel as the members departed. She conjured up three further cups of tea for us in the small back kitchen of the church hall.

She persuaded me to share my burden. I sniffed. "There's been a most unfortunate event at the funeral service held earlier today when the widower Elwyn Morgan, of Orielton Farm was being laid to rest in Monkton cemetery!" I paused; the other women let me take my time. We all knew that if a good story needs to be told then it needs time to be told well.

I continued. "All had run smoothly through the funeral service. I stepped forward to perform my last duty before the coffin was lowered for the final internment. I removed the British Legion flag which had been draped over the coffin, Elwyn was a great supporter of the army during the war you know, he supplied the entire Castlemartin camp with the best prime beef and lamb cuts you could imagine, right through rationing never missed a day."

I waited for them to take in the importance of Elwyn's contribution to the war effort, I went on. "As I was folding the flag, staring up at me in all their brass engraved brilliance were the words – In Loving memory of our beloved Gwendolyn Alys Rogers, 1863 – 1953."

Carol from Chapel whispered. "You were about to intern Gwennie from Railway Terrace into the Elwyn Morgan family plot?"

I dropped my chin. "Just about the most dreadful act that any undertaker could perform. Except of course losing the odd body or two, but that's a different story. I stopped the service there and then and we took Gwennie back to the Chapel of Rest."

I could almost hear Bessie's brain churning as she pointed us towards the likely causes of such a calamity. "Who draped the coffin, and when?"

I wiped away an imaginary tear, not a lot of room for genuine misting over in my profession. "It was my doing, I always sort out the coffin covers and wreaths with the family well in advance I draped the flag over Elwyn's coffin late last night. I always make sure that the corner pleats are tidy. Someone must have moved it over onto Gwennie's coffin."

Carol observed. "They would know that you would have seen it at the graveside, what was the purpose of causing such an upset not to mention you having to do it all over again."

I took comfort from Carol. "That's true, the next available booking in Monkton church is next week. The poor family, thankfully there are only two of them left, will have to stand out in the cold again to pay their final respects."

Bessie raised a hand. "Truth be told, there are three of them left in that family, the younger boy left under a bit of a cloud seven years ago to settle abroad. The older son and his sister are working the farm."

One of Bessie's many strengths was that she never liked to gossip unless it was for the good of all concerned. She explained to us,

"It was during the time that Elwyn was in hospital during a spell of recurring gout. It would seem to be that a large sum of money had gone missing from the kitchen dresser and all the evidence pointed

40

towards the youngest of Elwyn's three children – Gareth. The investigating officer, Sergeant Evans," as was her way she was quick to use her husband's official rank, "wasn't convinced of the boy's guilt and because Elwyn didn't want people to know they had quite a bit money under the mattress, so to speak, they hushed it all up. My husband recommended that the boy, however innocent, would be best creating a tidy distance from himself and the farm. He certainly took the Sergeant's advice and set off for Australia before his father had returned from hospital. No one in the town has heard from him since."

I looked up. "I didn't know the details of the family row, it's never come up in my dealings with them. The poor boy doesn't even know that his father has passed on. Even with jet planes and all, he'd take a week or so to get back home."

Bessie stood up and took our empty cups to the sink, she said over her shoulder. "Coming back to the switched flag, could we pop in for a cup of tea during the week for you to show us around? We might be able to shed some light on your misfortune today. Thinking about things, apart from a very unhappy family and extra work for you Myvvi, I can't see the point of it all. Would your husband mind if we popped in when you haven't got appointments?"

I smiled for the first time all afternoon. "I'll be happier when I've booked in Elwyn's second attempt to be interned, I'm sure a brief service at the graveside would be acceptable to his remaining relatives. I would love to know what went wrong and my husband would welcome a visit from the living for a change."

***

All that was left of my generous slices of homemade fruit cake was a small circle of crumbs which Bessie had tidied up into the middle of the plate. In between several half-finished coffins stacked against the front wall was a long bench made of a wide selection of colourful timber offcuts ranging from beech through oak to yew; my husband often bemoaned that his timber supplier would only drop off a standard size length when delivering his order taking no consideration in the least of the length of the coffin's intended occupant. The bench was usually utilised by the town's elderly population taking a breather, as they went about their daily trawl for news, gossip and myth all in one conversation. The bench was tentatively referred to as the funeral parlour's waiting room.

The morbid description held no sway with the four of us sat on the bench, sipping our tea and looking out over the town quay across the river to where the coastal schooner – The Kathleen and May, so named after the Irish owner's daughters, was discharging its cargo of coal and cement. Watching other people at work has the same fascination worldwide Bessie observed as she turned to me,

"Thank you very much for your very interesting tour of the funeral parlour and in particular the room where departing coffins are prepared for the hearse. What you could describe as the scene of the crime. We've all enjoyed your hospitality including Beryl the Will alongside me, whom you kindly welcomed after I had suggested that she may be able to enhance our findings today."

I took the compliment without blushing; I had catered in the past for many more. I was no stranger to wakes attended by hundreds and was no longer amazed at how much people can eat even at the height of their bereavement.

Beryl piped up. "I met Bessie coming out of the Station Road stores and she told me about your bother at the graveyard. If it's any consolation, my husband, Elwyn's solicitor, has had to cancel a golf match at Tenby later this week to read the will. One of the conditions it seems is that it can only be read and executed the day after Mr Morgan has finally been put to rest. I just hope that all will go well at the churchyard this time and that no one else will be inconvenienced."

Carol the Chapel concurred. "The only outcome from all of this is that the funeral has been delayed for a few days, it makes me wonder why did the person who switched the flag over even bother."

"Exactly," echoed Bessie. "Why did they come through the open back door into the Chapel of Rest? Myvvi here has told us that it's her practice to leave it unlocked all night in case a bereaved family member decides to hold a farewell vigil. How would they know? Most of all, who would know besides the undertaker, Myvvi and the bearers when they collected the coffin that it was the one draped in the British Legion flag."

Beryl had a logical way about her. "I don't think we are going to find the answer here at the funeral parlour, we need to go up to the farm."

I contributed. "I've got to go up tomorrow after they have finished morning milking to go through the shortened service to be conducted at the internment, could one of you come along and do a bit of ferreting?"

Beryl smiled. "I have never let a ferret go near my fingers in all my life but a couple of well-placed questions might tell us more."

Carol said. "There's a problem with the music at chapel which needs my attention. Trev the organist says it's nothing to do with him or the organ. He says just because he and the organ are both seventy, neither of them is past it. I'll catch up with you girls at our next meeting."

I started to stack the cups up. "If that's alright with you Bessie, I'll take Beryl up to Orielton tomorrow then."

Bessie replied. "Couldn't agree more with you girl, wouldn't want to alert anyone of our suspicions. I'm more than happy for you two to find, all there is to be found out, on that farm."

***

I parked my spotless and gleaming Hillman Minx two hundred yards from the farm gate. I was under strict instructions from my husband to ensure that our immaculate vehicle, second in radiance only to the hearse, should not encounter a single memento of the visit to the farm. Beryl and I confirmed our responsibilities as we walked around the farmhouse towards the milking shed. The older son John was cleaning out after the morning milking leaving their twelve cows to make their well-trodden way back down to the meadow. The daughter Elen was carrying two pails of milk into the dairy. As agreed, I had decided to change my court shoes for wellington boots and braved the pervading countryside aroma emerging from the milking shed to go through the details of the amended funeral service with John. I asked if Elen would be so good as to explain to Beryl, a bit of a town girl, how they made the best butter in Pembrokeshire. The visit was over in next to no time and we were comparing notes as I drove back to the funeral parlour taking the longer route via Maiden Wells and St Daniel's Hill.

"What a misery!" I described John Morgan to Beryl. "He barely looked at the order of service and complained that through my incompetence it was taking far too long to commit his father into the ground. He said that he was in two minds to ask the funeral directors in Pembroke Dock to take the whole thing over. I had to explain to him that professional etiquette prevents such an exchange between undertakers. To pass the dearly departed over the garden fence so to speak, was disrespectful to the recently passed and harrowing to most members of the family. He finally said he couldn't wait for the funeral to be done with."

"I'm so sorry that you had to be on the receiving end of all that," commiserated Beryl. "Elen was a little nervous at first but I think my inventive townie questions like why isn't milk green after the cows eat tons of grass made her smile, she then relaxed and gave me a bit of an insight to what is going on but it will, unfortunately, bring you and me more grief before this entire matter is laid to rest." Beryl allowed herself a little smile at her unintentional choice of words.

I sighed. "It sounds as if you've unearthed something," we both smiled at my funereal pun. "At this rate, I'll be taking a ten-mile detour around Penally and Tenby to get the facts from you, but if we are at last making some sense of this at all please continue."

Beryl drew in a deep breath, her preference to say less and achieve more was about to be tested. "The old man missed the younger son a great deal. He was his favourite for sure and neither he nor Elen ever doubted Gareth's innocence. Elen said that he looked down the lane every morning to see if his prodigal son was returning. He never gave up hope that Gareth would come back. She thinks Elwyn died of a broken heart. Eventually, Elen found herself looking down towards the main road every day."

Beryl swallowed. "She appears to believe that Gareth will return to the farm someday. She wouldn't say how it would happen. Elen more than anyone wanted to delay the funeral, she confessed to me that she had been nearly out of her mind when she crept into your Chapel of Rest and moved the flag over, she was desperate to prevent the funeral from going ahead. By now, having admitted what she had done, she had become a little tearful, I made her stand back from the butter pats she was making and calmed her down. I said that as far as all the cases my husband had dealt with as a solicitor, none of them had attached a custodial sentence for interfering with a funeral. I left matters there, but I gleaned that all of this would come out at the reading of the will. She then added that her older brother could be very moody and asked me if my being the executor's wife would prevent me from attending as a witness. I didn't want to go through the facts around witnesses being usually involved much earlier in the will proceedings so I said I could be invited as a new-found family friend. I agreed to come out with my husband the day after the funeral.

I changed down a gear to tackle the steep hill approaching the Ridgeway. "Well done, you seem to have helped her get through her difficult time and gained her confidence, not least of all our coffin-switching mystery has been solved"

Beryl briefly touched my arm. "I wish that was all, Elen has asked that the funeral be delayed by one more day, she says it will make a tremendous difference to her for the rest of her life.

I made a face. "It'll shorten mine when my husband finds out."

Beryl made her plea. "I believe the girl is trying to do what's right by her late father, we ought to help her out. You say yours will be upset; my husband will go straight up in the air just like one of his bad golf shots. Let's take a stand for this young woman, after all she lost her mother when she was very young and now, she is fatherless."

I sighed. "They say the living are a bigger nuisance than the dead, I can only agree, but I'll tell you now girl, I'm not looking forward to explaining this entire drama to the Sewing Circle at our next meeting."

I drove on, more to the point, how was I going to avoid being banned for life from Monkton church and cemetery for subjecting the vicar to a string of incomplete funeral services.

Beryl said. "My more immediate challenge is what treat I can offer my husband for dinner before I ruin his appetite for a pudding when I tell him the reading of the will is to be delayed by another day. She looked down the hill, saw the beach and the sea and said to me. "Well I never, however did we get to Saundersfoot?"

✳✳✳

Beryl and I took shelter from the incoming breeze behind the coffins stacked up outside our workshop on the quay. We sipped our tea and watched the Kathleen and May coastal schooner slip her moorings and take the late morning tide down the estuary towards the Cleddau river and the open Irish sea.

Beryl was explaining how she had followed her preference to say little or nothing when a difference of opinion with her husband was being aired,

"As you know the funeral went ahead yesterday without any late obstruction or misfortune. We were having breakfast this morning before going out for the reading of the will when we received a brief but mournful call from the call-box outside the farm – it was Elen. She pleaded for the will reading to be moved to the afternoon. Any plans for my husband's recreational relaxation were thrown out with the uneaten rashers of best Welsh bacon and rapidly curling toast. He stormed out to conduct a half-day of work at the town hall complaining bitterly, 'What is the point of living close to the oldest golf course in Wales if you are being constantly prevented from even getting to the first tee?'"

I responded. "I still have some personal effects to give back to Elen, I can give you a lift out there, it will save you a silent journey with your husband and he can depart for the golf course directly after the reading. From what you've said Elen sounded quite upset this morning, she will probably welcome support from the both of us."

***

I parked my car a respectable distance behind the Mark Six Bentley carefully positioned well away from the overgrown hedge and any natural manure deposits along the approach lane to the farm.

Elen came out to greet us; she was wearing a big smile and a floral dress with her hair tied back neatly. I barely recognised her from the country girl complete with farm-worn dungarees and oversized wellington boots on our previous encounter.

Elen explained that she had taken charge of Beryl's husband on his arrival and that he was being consoled for his inconveniences by taking a cup of tea along with home-cooked Welsh cakes and butter made on the premises.

I wondered what had got into the girl. The enthusiasm with which she was propelling us towards the farmhouse kitchen was well beyond any character traits she'd displayed in the short time since Beryl and I had known her.

The mountain of Welsh cakes presented to Beryl's husband was gratefully received as an opportune replacement for his lost breakfast. He had eventually managed to steady the continuous cups of tea and suggested that the time had arrived for the formal reading of the will. John, without a word to match his surly look, was first to sit down in the front parlour, his impatience plain for all to see. I noticed that Elen was watching the grandfather clock in the corner and visibly relaxed as the chimes confirmed it was four o'clock.

The first part of the will had been read. Donations to several animal charities and a fund desperate to attend to the leaks in the roof of Monkton church had been announced.

I was beginning to think that the problem with this will, had been more in the arrangement of the reading rather than in the content itself when a strong knock on the door jamb behind us, made everyone look around. A smiling sun-tanned face greeted us. "G'day all, it's been a real bludger of a trip, seven days on the road or up in the air to be deadset."

Elen gave a squeal. "At last!" she jumped up and threw herself into what I could only surmise was her brother's arms. They finally disentangled and Elen took Gareth by the hand to sit next to her on the settee. The reading of the will continued. The list of local societies receiving funds became lengthy ending only when the local temperance society had received its modest legacy. I had noticed the half-full bottles of spirits inside the glass door of the bookcase and drew the conclusion that Elwyn had been following the temperance edict for moderation rather than absolute abstinence.

Beryl's husband coughed, it brought me back into the present, it seemed to me that an announcement of some import was about to be made.

He coughed again before announcing that the farm and its entirety had been left to Elen and John. Elwyn's life savings, which would be found in a large biscuit tin up on the rafters of the barn was to be given to Gareth but only if he'd returned to the farm before the will had been executed. The old man in his latter years hadn't given up the hope of his youngest son setting foot again on the soil of his birthright. The will was folded up and placed back in Beryl's husband's black briefcase.

John stood up, he seemed more relieved now that everything was out in the open. "Those cows won't milk themselves," he looked at Elen and Gareth and said gruffly. "You two can catch up with things if you want to, I've got a dairy farm to run." He left, leaving a distinct trail of mud from his ex-army boots all the way up the passageway.

Beryl's husband bid his goodbyes and disappeared up the lane.

She said. "I think it's only fair that we are given some kind of explanation, don't you?"

The reunion of the siblings was in full flow when I asked. "Elen, we can see that you and Gareth have a lot to catch up on, we won't intrude. We would like to know though, how you managed to bring Gareth home."

Following a nod of concurrence from her brother Elen explained. "The moment that Gareth was settled in Australia, he sent me a letter marked 'to be handed to the addressee only.' Our postie knew what was going on, not many British stamps carried a kangaroo. It was clear to him and me that Gareth didn't want to upset our father anymore. We have written several times a year and it wasn't long before I was able to confirm that the previous biscuit tin had been hidden out in the barn for safekeeping by my father while he was in hospital. I asked Gareth if he wanted to come back but," she put her hand on her brother's arm, "he said he was making a new life and it was best to leave some stones unturned. I sent him a telegram when father passed away but between getting himself onto a flight, and avoiding flooded runways at Karachi, I think it was, he was being held up all the way here. He even missed the train from Paddington and sent a telegram to the Postie to tell me he wouldn't be here until this afternoon. Dad had told me what was in the will, I wanted to put a great wrong right and for Gareth to be here to claim his rightful inheritance." Elen sat back with nothing further to say.

"Our presence here has served its purpose," said Beryl, she stood and waited for me to join her by the door. Elen hugged us and sent us both down the lane clutching a bag of Welsh cakes. As it happened it was a quiet journey back to town. I thought that Beryl might be wondering how her husband's delayed golf match was going and whether he would have room for more Welsh cakes after his dinner this evening.

I was dealing with the emerging problem of reporting back the tumultuous events of the last few days to the eager and all-listening ladies of the Station Road Sewing Circle.

Grown from Seed – *Maria from Milan*

I was the latest recruit to the Station Road Sewing Circle and as I had hoped I had been made more than welcome. Since my move from Milan to Pembroke to join my husband in one of the Kingsbridge cottages below Holyland Woods, I had been shown nothing but kindness. I in turn had, worked hard to learn English, in particular the Pembroke version. Despite it being spoken locally with a broad West Wales accent, compounded by the legacy of invading Normans and their Flemish artisans many centuries earlier, my efforts were almost understood.

My husband Antonio had spent a small part of his army service in a prisoner of war camp north of Haverfordwest. He had earned the respect of many for his industrious approach to his work and for gaining a passable vocabulary. He had decided to return to Pembrokeshire to set up an ice cream parlour, which our friends had said during their frequent trips back to Italy, was the biggest growing industry in the popular holiday county. He had no trouble at all in securing the position of milkman with Georgie Rossiter of Lordsacre farm. If I say it to myself, Antonio's warm personality has endeared him to all on his delivery round. I felt that him being a milkman was clearly a stepping stone on his journey to introduce the people of Pembroke to Neapolitan ice cream delights.

All that said, he wasn't a happy man. For the second year in a row, he was having huge problems growing his pumpkins from seed. He told me most days that he didn't know how to make them – well, huge. I had heard in a previous sewing circle meeting three women discussing pumpkins and how they blighted everyday life for at least two months of every year. I joined them at their table more in hope of helping my Antonio than by intent.

Joan the Tip looked bothered. "We've all been through this before. It's getting so bad now that he drives the dustbin lorry down to the allotments before he gets home for his tea. The poor people in nearby Woodbine Terrace think they have missed a bin-day and rush through their houses to put their dustbins out."

Megan the Signals agreed. "It's every year, you can see it coming by looking at the calendar, eight weeks of absolute misery. He doesn't do a thing around our cottage behind the Signal-box, even though there are only six trains a day passing through. Every spare minute he has he uses to go down the greenhouse and talk to his latest treasures."

Maggie the Shop could only concur. "When you think they are only good for making a lantern or a pie, the pumpkins that is, not our husbands, they certainly take over in the weeks leading up to the Pembroke Flower and Vegetable show. There could be a queue out the door of the shop and down the Main Street and where would he be? Down the bottom of our garden in his pumpkin patch!"

"Be fair ladies," I found myself joining in. "You might lose your husbands for a little while but between them, they are likely to carry off the top prizes. My Antonio is doing his best but his pumpkins seem to have stopped growing. Most Saturdays when he's collecting the milk money, he comes home even more downhearted after meeting your husband on the doorstep. They can only talk, about whether they will win the first, second or third prize, Antonio would settle for a Highly Commended award any year."

Joan responded. "Our sewing circle stands for fairness, it's not right that Maria is taking the consequences of our husbands' boastful claims. We will have to help Antonio, who now you mention it, hasn't been that chirpy for a while."

Megan spoke up. "If there was only a way that my husband could be persuaded to give up a secret or two. It could help Antonio to achieve his cherished Highly Commended award."

I tilted my chin. "That's very kind of you to offer but I know that your men are all striving for the top place, the last thing they would agree to is to give anything away."

Maggie was smiling. "What if they thought that they were gaining an advantage over their nearest rivals?"

Both Joan and Megan were now beaming.

Megan spoke out. "This sounds like one of your schemes Maggie; to get your husband to do something he would never do, we can't wait to hear it."

Maggie put her needle-point map of Pembroke back into her sewing box and took out a small notebook complete with pencil. "We've been bored over the years listening to how our men believe that they would win the first prize for their pumpkins. I think we can put our suffering to good use. We must convince them that we have unknowingly handed them an assured victory over each other. They will then be more inclined to help Antonio, who after all, they will never see as a threat."

She licked the end of her pencil. "Let's write down the things we can remember they did to their pumpkins during the past few years. We'll then produce an almost identical list to put in front of them. By next week we should know how Antonio can get himself back into the frame, so to speak."

I sat back, watched the three animated women construct their list and wondered if it could ever be used to restore my Antonio to his former good-natured self.

✳✳✳

I had invited my three friends to come to tea at my home in Kingsbridge cottages.

Whilst my favoured afternoon drink is well-brewed Italian coffee, I had learned in sewing circle meetings that if you constantly sip tea you wouldn't have to put up with the full taste of it. I set out two plates, one loaded with my Milanese favourite Panettone; I know this tall cake should be served at Christmas but we were in the middle of an emergency. The other carried a Cassata alla Sicilione, a cheesecake from the other end of Italy. The groans of their reluctant appetites gave me hope that as soon as the plates were empty, we would be making progress towards my husband's well-being.

Joan the Tip was first to report her findings,

"I had started to have our evening meal later to fit in with his trips to the allotment after work. My husband said that it was good, that I was for a change, helping him to walk off with the challenge cup. I reminded him that it was about time that he had won, but I understood that the other two boys always had a trick or two up their sleeves.

He even stopped reading the back pages of the Western Telegraph when I said that I was wondering if he could help one of the ladies in our sewing circle whose husband is down in the dumps with his pumpkins."

I interrupted her, alarmed I was. "Did you say it was my husband? That would embarrass him to know we were helping him out."

Joan smiled. "I definitely didn't, but I knew from my husband's expression that he had worked out it was Antonio, after all, there were only four entries in that competition last year. When I said we had written down a few things from memory, which didn't amount to much, he couldn't wait to see the list.

Maggie leaned forward. "Did anything catch his eye?"

"He asked me who had written down about growing pumpkins in a dustbin, I said I thought it had been you, it was something your husband had tried but it hadn't come to much."

Megan was wiping crumbs from her lips after a late assault on the Panettone. "Did you get anything out of him?"

"By now he had put his coat on saying he had to go over the allotment to check something out. I asked him straight out, are you going to help my friend or not?"

Joan paused, I was shaking with anticipation before she concluded,

"He said I should ask her if her husband had been using Georgie Rossiter's free cow manure. That could be his problem. It's a much better texture from a horse. Without so much as a see you later, he was out the door.

Maggie asked. "So what did you do then?"

Joan beamed. "I went into the back scullery and made myself a celebratory cup of tea. - mission accomplished."

We all sat back, smiled and waited for the next revelation.

Megan the Signals responded. "I had to corner my husband in his greenhouse when I knew very well that the last train on the up line from Pembroke Dock to Carmarthen was due in only six minutes. I wedged myself in the doorway determined that I wasn't going to move until I had an answer."

I had this image in front of me of Megan, by no means a stick of a girl, completely blocking the exit from the greenhouse. Immovable or what?

She continued. "I asked him for the second time for a helping hand not even that, one single finger's worth of assistance for my friend at our sewing circle. He was on his knees turning his pumpkin around a measured amount while being so he said careful not to put any tension into the vine. He said his prize-destined entry would greet the morning sun, so positioned to be ripening the yellow and gold skin evenly across its surface. He was a bit short with me saying, I haven't the time to stop and look at any list if you please, I must finish adjusting my beautiful pumpkin to ensure that she will be evenly radiant on the day.

I stayed true to my waiting game, saying I do understand your passion for pumpkins, I might even give you a divorce so that you can propose marriage to one. All I need now, well – in the next five minutes, is a bit of kindness towards my friend's husband. He made a small final adjustment and stood up saying, read your list out to me as we walk up to the signal box and I'll tell you when you've reached a suitable suggestion. I didn't move. Instead, I replied that he'll get to the signal box in under four minutes if he would look at the list and pick one out. Between me not moving and the fast-approaching train he gave in.

He snatched the list from me and put it in his pocket saying, Won't be much on here that you and the girls have come up with. He then said the oddest thing."

Just when I was wondering if Megan had learned anything at all, her well-placed pause brought me back to her conclusion. The women of Pembroke know for sure how to tell a story.

"He said simply, your friend's husband's best bet is to use Epsom salts. I was livid, I said in the next three minutes if you haven't cleared the signal, you'll become the most disgraced signalman in the history of West Wales. Is all you can suggest that her husband's upset stomach is the reason he can't grow pumpkins?"

At last, he was getting desperate, he gasped

"Not for him I mean - for the pumpkin look you. Diluted with

54

water and sprayed on the leaves the salts will give it the magnesium it needs to grow."

I moved swiftly to one side; my husband sprinted up the path towards the signal box. His reputation would still be intact. It was only then that I wondered how you other ladies were getting on."

Megan leaned back, then looked with intent towards the remaining slices of Cassata. I offered a fresh cup of tea before we heard from Maggie the Shop. I went into my small kitchen to put the kettle on. I tried to tell myself that a bucket of horse manure and a dose of Epsom salts was a sound basis for my Antonio to grow his pumpkins on. Truth be told, my hopes were now pinned on the last to speak and her entertaining way of telling a story. Well known for her pantomime scripts, I had heard that she reports most of her written information as if every conversation were to be performed on the stage.

Maggie turned her cup over, signalling that when this part was well and truly done, there would be a spot of tea-leaf reading to follow. She pulled out several sheets of typed paper from her handbag and handed us a copy each. She then read,

Operation Pumpkin
Maggie the Shop enters from a stockroom. (She is fed up),

Maggie
Have you looked at the note we spoke about, I left it for you in the till this morning?

Husband
Can't say I have Cariad! (He speaks with a North Wales accent)

Maggie
You won't get around me with your Welsh words of affection, why haven't you read it?

Husband
I've been rushed off my feet this morning. We've been selling bags of flour and packets of dried fruit like hot cakes you see. (Smiles at own words)
Truth be told it's all down to that latest new Betty Crocker publication they've got in the library. Bron the Books was in earlier, she wasn't very happy. The book is permanently out on loan and she said it's been coming back covered with so many ingredients you might as well put it in the oven and bake it.

Maggie

Too true, and with all the street parties being planned for the Coronation we'd better double our order at the wholesaler. However, before all that you've got a flower and vegetable show to prepare for, how are your pumpkins coming along?

Husband

Very nicely indeed, I will be giving those other two a good run for their money.

Maggie

Look now Mr Bentley, the shop will be full of customers before we know it. All being intent on baking enough cake to feed the first battalion of the Welsh Guards. Kindly take the list out of the till, which one of those methods, used by the three of you, would help my friend's husband to achieve a highly commended card?

Husband

(Reading down list pausing every few lines to look up at door for customers, he scratches his head.)

Two things, what does the word colouring mean with respect to pumpkins? they produce their own colour - yellow and gold."

Maggie

Joan the Tip put that down, apparently one year her husband hadn't turned his pumpkin enough to ripen, he tried a bit of food colouring on the back of it to bring it up to scratch. He didn't win that year.

(She waits for his second point).

Husband

Nothing on here will help anyone with the show only four weeks away. Not that I'm saying I've a good idea who this is all about but he could try scattering his Italian coffee grounds all around the pumpkin and water them in.

Maggie

Is that it then, with all your experience you want me to pass on that he should pour his coffee dregs all over his pumpkin?"

Husband

My Dearest, Fy Anwylaf, let me finish. He needs to empty his coffee pot into a watering can, mix it with water and spray the ground around the vine. It'll get a nice boost of nitrogen."

(Mrs Llewellyn times her entrance well; clutching a flour-stained, well-thumbed *and generally battered book. By the time she reaches the counter she is pointing at the shelf containing her desired ingredients.)*

Maggie

I'll get the sultanas my Cariad and bring them over.
(Then murmurs) True love can indeed move mountains, never mind pumpkins.

Before we had all folded up our scripts, I had all I needed to cheer my husband up.

I asked. "Ladies, should we see if the tea leaves can confirm that we will have better days ahead?"

***

The four of us were walking in the strong afternoon sun. joined it seems by half the town who were heading up Station Road to the show field. I could hear the shouts of the winners on the sideshows and the squeals of the more adventurous on the rides. Our determined path led us through the field gate and past the queues of excited children. We moved without deflection towards the marquee with the large sign draped across it – The Vegetable Exhibits.

Joan the Tip was the first to speak as we stopped short of the entrance. "He's been up here all day, mind you. He looked worried when he left first thing. it must be something to do with the wooden water butt that he sawed in half. He kept saying that no one would run circles around him this year."

Megan the Signals chipped in. "I've never seen mine looking so full of himself, he's been like it since he went down to Beddoe's the Ironmongers and staggered home with their entire stock of fine sandpaper. I could hardly move in my kitchen for opened sandpaper wrappers all over the place."

Maggie the Shop said. "My husband has been humming 'Men of Harlech' without stopping for breath for the last two weeks. He thinks I haven't noticed that two small bottles of cochineal are missing, you know, they add it to icing sugar to spruce up a birthday cake. I only noticed it because we hardly ever sell yellow or gold for decoration."

I didn't say anything. My Antonio had been his normal happy self

57

after I had accidentally left the list on the kitchen table. Maggie had written the growing suggestions in capital letters giving me no trouble in adding the three suggestions received from their husbands at the bottom.

From the moment that Antonio started to treat his pumpkin with gallons of Epsom salts, loads of horse manure and countless coffee leftovers, it had more than doubled in size. Even if it would never reach the full size of a champion, I was sure that he would carry off his longed-for highly commended card.

We went through the flap and caught the first whiff of trouble. It was roasting; the unseasonal sun and the judges' omission to lift the flaps after their appraisal of all entries, away from prying eyes, had made the vegetable tent a Turkish bath. We approached the pumpkin table and a woman stood there transfixed. Carnage wouldn't even begin to describe the sight before us.

The first pumpkin was perfectly round and looked in every way to be a winning effort. Provided that is, if you didn't look too closely at the bruises and gouges that ran around its middle. The only explanation that Joan could offer was that it had been prised out of the bottom half of a water butt in either haste or frustration.

The second magnificent entry was sat in a large pool of pumpkin juice which was still seeping through its shiny, smooth but plainly wafer-thin skin. Without a doubt, the temperature in the tent had a great deal to answer for. Megan said it would be best if she cleared the pile of sandpaper wrappings away before her husband returned home.

The most spectacular tragedy had clearly occurred to the third pumpkin in the row. Even though the lights were on in the tent the pumpkin had a distinct glow about it. The streaks of bright yellow and vivid gold spreading up from its base were gleaming, giving the whole plant a metallic appearance.

Maggie whispered that she wished she had told her husband that the food colouring was luminous.

I couldn't move. I stood in front of the modest offering on the end plinth. Whilst smaller than the previous exhibits I thought it looked a picture of a pumpkin to use one of Antonio's descriptions that he'd read out to me from the Gardener's Weekly.

Our shocked eyes moved downwards together.

The three largest entries carried a white Highly Commended card. The slightly smaller pumpkin had been awarded First prize, a red card complete, with a silver cup.

I had to draw their attention from the heart-rending scenes before them. "Where are they?"

Maggie turned and headed for the entrance flap. "The only place they'll be is in the beer tent drowning each other's sorrows."

We pushed our way through the swelling crowds in an unstoppable straight-line formation directly to the open-sided marquee emblazoned with a no-nonsense banner – Beer Sold Here!

Joan saw them first; she stopped dead and we cannoned into the back of her. She pointed to the four men standing around a table. It was strewn with empty glasses and each of them was carrying a full glass in their hands. They were roaring with laughter, slapping each other on the back only stopping to repeatedly clink their glasses with Antonio and congratulate him. He was grinning so much that he was holding the side of his face. We went over to the table and stood shoulder to shoulder waiting for an explanation.

Maggie's husband appeared to be on shandies and had therefore been appointed the spokesman. "It was like this, without admitting anything mark you. One of us made grooves in his pumpkin when getting it out of its growing container, another had made his pumpkin's surface too smooth to be good. As for the third entry, the heavy application of colouring which glows in the dark turned out the lights for its grower. While Antonio's entry wasn't the biggest it was perfectly formed in all of the judges' eyes. When we realised that our rivalry had caused us to stray off the straight and narrow and we'd paid the consequences we could see the funny side of it."

Megan asked. "Didn't the judges have anything to say about your antics?"

Her husband put his arm around Antonio's shoulder. "We need to thank Mr Antonio Marinacci here, he suggested to them that our little problems had come out solely from seeking perfection. The judges accepted his good-natured plea without a murmur."

Maggie's husband picked up his glass saying. "Let's toast our Italian friend and hope that he doesn't enter next year!"

Joan said. "We'd be delighted to join you as soon as one of you men can get yourselves over to the bar."

I ran over and threw my arms around Antonio's neck crying. "That's my Boyo!"

When the laughter had died down, Maggie said. "Hark at her, she'll be more Welsh than Italian by the time they open up their ice cream parlour.

Stepping out Nicely – *Auntie Sian*

Now, I loves a tidy shoe. Not only the pairs that I frequently buy in town that have caught my eye for modern fashion with a nice fit but the sets of four which my nephew the blacksmith, made and fitted to many of the horses within the Pembroke district. I'll admit to being usually proud beyond myself of the quality and modest pricing of his Smithy-made shoes, but on this occasion, I have nothing good to say about them.

"They are worrying the poor boy off his food." I was confiding to Glenys the Coal, in the weekly meeting of the Station Road Sewing Circle. "He has queues of horse owners going back up the Lamphey Road, including Wednesday mind you, which they all know is his day to work on his overdue ornamental gates."

Glenys frowned. "That doesn't sound very worrying to me, he should be pleased that his business is expanding!"

"That's my point girl," I insisted. "it's the queues that are growing; the business is shrinking. My nephew told me that some customers are coming back for new shoes to be fitted well before their due time. It takes him the best part of a morning to fit a new set on a shire horse you see and if anyone returns with worn or lost shoes within the agreed time, he promised to give them a free set. In a sentence - He's working for nothing. What's worse, a couple of them have said if he doesn't get a handle on it soon, they'll be moving to the Smithy in Manorbier."

Glenys's frown hadn't moved much. "I think we need to have a few more facts before I can see how we can help your nephew."

I sighed. "Now there's another problem, you see. You know that I brought him up after his mother ran off with that carpet salesman from Blackwood Mon. The Welshman wasn't up to much but she wanted a life with a thick woollen pile under her feet. The boy's father, my late brother, didn't want to know him so I brought him up and made him very independent. He's not only the proud owner of the Smithy; he'll not want to accept help from the likes of us."

Glenys looked as if she was finished with listening. "Now look here Auntie Sian, we are very much the kind of help he needs and better still he won't even know about it. Our sewing circle does its real work on the quiet, I think you and me need to go on a fact-gathering mission before we share these goings on with any of the others."

Glenys the Coal took my watery smile as an acceptance and outlined her plan. "You will, with great care, pop into the Smithy to see how things are going. Take him a sandwich and offer to make him a cup of tea. While you're waiting for the kettle to boil, make a copy of the entries in his work ledger. Your nephew won't notice; he'll be busy dealing with his dissatisfied customers. We need to see if any pattern can be determined from the notes he's added during this troubling time."

I was feeling a bit happier now that I was doing something. Glenys was up and running by now. "I'll see what I can find out too." She added.

I didn't understand. "How will you do that then?"

"First, I will drop in for a cup of tea with a selection of my husband's customers along the Lamphey Road. It's close to the Smithy and they'll have a thing or two to say about queues of horses outside their houses. Not to mention the rose fertiliser they've left behind! I will also conduct an extended loiter outside Mrs Foreman's sweet shop on Station Road. I'll be sure to capture any unusual happenings in the roads approaching the shop or the smithy for that matter."

Due to the seriousness of the impact on my nephew's business and the shortage of time, I suggested that we met in Brown's café in two days to compare our findings. Glenys said that this mystery will take some unravelling so we'd better get there early – to get a seat next to the ice cream machine.

∗∗∗

62

As I had hoped Brown's café had started to empty of the early morning trade, among the exceptions were the town's three postmen. They always took their first tea break in the café as soon as they had stepped out of the Post Office next door before they went on their rounds. You could barely get in the door for mailbags. When all is said and done, their words not mine, delivering Her Majesty's mail was indeed thirsty work. Further testament to this point of view was their getting together right after their rounds, for a mid-afternoon stiffener in the Hope Inn on East End Square.

I waited for the four Provident cheque door-knockers to depart. They had travelled down from Swansea in the same Morris Minor. I saw it parked outside. A carefully torn-up street map of Pembroke was on the table in front of them about to be shared. Each piece set out the patch they needed to cover that day. I was pleased to see them set off with their false promises neatly folded into their smart imitation-leather briefcases.

Considering it was still quite early, Glenys and me surprised ourselves by finishing off a vanilla wafer and a chocolate sundae before I brought our little meeting to order.

I went first,

"I managed to make a copy of his workbook and having had a good look; I can confirm that it's only four horses that are involved so far in having their shoes replaced for free. Perhaps I was a bit carried away when I said the queue was up the road. All four of them are over sixteen hands and they were shod for fieldwork."

Glenys intervened. "I think you'd better run that past me in English, slow Welsh if you'd like, but that's a bit too technical."

I started again. "The horses are stabled in two places. One at the bottom of St Daniel's Hill and three in a field on the other side of the Pembroke cricket pitch on the Lamphey road. They are all big Shires and their backs are over six feet off the ground. If such a horse is used for working in the field, then they have a softer metal shoe fitted. If the Shire is doing roadwork all day long, like Georgie Rossiter's Lucy, on her milk round, they have a harder shoe on them. Road shoes are much more expensive. My Nephew's notes said that for the shoes to have worn so quickly the owners must have been using them on the road and had taken the softer shoes to save money at the discomfort

63

of their horse. They deny anything of the sort."

Glenys retorted. "Him being outspoken and all, there's a good argument in the making. It's a wonder they've come back at all."

"You're too right girl," I nodded,

I waited for Glenys to get on with her report.

"This is what I've found out, it may be something or nothing. In between putting away a couple of buckets of tea with the coal customers, I spent quite a bit of time filling myself with Pontefract cakes outside Mrs Foreman's sweet shop when I met the Vicar's wife, Mrs Branston-Phelps, you know from the Vicarage at the top of the First Lane. I walked her home to get every bit of her story. She simply said – I never used to believe in ghosts but this is the third time in as many weeks that the Ghost of Hywel the Highwayman has returned to haunt me!"

I perked up on being reminded of the infamous son of Pembroke who had been making his escape from the constabulary galloping through Holyland woods when a low branch took his head off. They found his body but the head has never been seen since. The legend is that he returns late at night to search for his head and regain his senses.

Glenys went on. "She had been staying up late to hear the bedtime thriller on the Light programme when she heard horse's hooves going up and down the lane. Every time she looked out the window though, the lane was empty." She sat back and drained her teacup waiting for me to make head or tail of it.

"Thinking about what we've found out so far," I observed, "there are horses who are going on the road who shouldn't be. Three of those horses are stabled down the road from the Vicarage. The vicar's wife is hearing things, not for the first time, she suffers with her nerves bless her and we are not much closer to saving my nephew's livelihood. Perhaps the horses escaped from their field and that's all there is to it. But something doesn't add up. I think we will have to call in on Bessie the Law on our way home to get her permission to send in the Night Owls."

"Couldn't agree with you more!" said Glenys licking her froth-covered spoon for the last time.

***

I waited until the tea had been sipped to the bottom of every cup in the church hall. Tea leaf readings had been conducted and communicated. The participants had been assured that it would be fine tomorrow and therefore ideal for sprucing up the children and visiting distant relatives. The cake crumbs had been daintily dusted from lips and vigorously brushed off plates. I was ready to introduce to the Station Road Sewing Circle the first report from the Night Owls. I gave a summary of our investigation so far, then nodded to Penny the Photo, a lovely girl, who without a smidgeon of self-awareness was showing off her model's figure in a hand-knitted Arran jumper. She had many attributes as her employer, Pugh the View – the town's photographer, would tell you, but her most valued talent from the sewing circle's point of view was that she didn't need much sleep. Taking her responsibility to the full as the Night Owl Leader she stood up,

"Following a thorough briefing from Auntie Sian and Glenys the Coal, me and Bron the Books set watch from midnight to three over the last few nights. I took the stable in Orange Gardens and I regret to say nothing happened except a fox walked by with a chicken in his mouth. I suspect he was on his way up St Daniel's hill with his family's dinner." She sat down.

Bron the Books, the remaining member of the Night Owls, stood up slowly, never one to rush things. If there was a queue out of the door of our library; she would still check every page of a returning book and issue on-the-spot fines for ripped, defaced or missing pages. Her suitability for being a night owl came from her love of reading. Truth be told, she once stayed up all night to finish The Long Goodbye by Raymond Chandler.

She was holding onto the table,

"I never have believed in ghosts," her voice wavered. "I still don't but I saw one last night."

As if tied together by the strongest sewing thread available ten women leaned forward in unison. Penny and I had already heard about Bron's haunting experience. She picked up her teacup and sipped the last of her tea, leaves and all I wouldn't be surprised.

She swallowed. "I took up my position behind the hedge at the corner of First Lane and Lamphey Road. I could see the stables where three of the shires were being kept and any movements up or down the main road. I was wearing my heavy black coat and settled down to read our best-seller, 'Ten quick ways to burn a Cake', a satire on domestic science in secondary schools. I was wearing my miner's lamp, strapped around my head, the light's a bit dim but alright to read by." She paused.

The women, who were barely sat in their chairs, waited. A sound build-up always proceeded a good story.

Bron continued. "I was deep in my book when I heard the clip-clop of a horse turning into the lane. I switched off my light, ran around to the gate and looked out. It was as plain as daylight even in the half moon. Trotting down the lane was a headless man on a large horse. I couldn't help noticing that he was nearly as broad as the horse itself. Before I could do anything more, he disappeared down the lane towards Kingsbridge and the Tenby Road."

She sat down and gratefully took a glass of water from Penny who had nipped out to the kitchen.

Bessie responded. "Well done girl, at least you have confirmed that the vicar's wife isn't giving in to her nerves. Before we decide on our next steps to help Sian's nephew does anyone have anything to add?"

Maria from Milan put one hand up, she was holding a battered horseshoe in the other.

"This horseshoe was the topic of a discussion between my husband Antonio and his employer Georgie Rossiter, the Midnight farmer. Georgie was about to mow his bottom meadow very early this morning and was walking the job, so to speak, when he picked up this large horseshoe. He said it was a field shoe and wanted to know where it had come from. He was annoyed to say the least because it could have damaged his mower and put him further behind in getting in the hay harvest."

Maria paused, she had already grasped how to insert silences into any conversation, to increase the impact of her spoken and occasional broken English.

"Antonio told him that someone must have thrown it into the field. Lucy wears road shoes and so it couldn't belong to her. Georgie was still unhappy, he said, 'There's a big horse out there, who could well be limping by now, the sooner that shoe is back on its hoof the better it will be for all concerned."

Bessie the Law thanked Maria for her contribution and then said. "Many of you will know that one of our many reliable sources of intelligence is the notebook belonging to my husband, Sergeant Evans. From time to time, I accidentally see some of the entries."

I smiled as the whole room did. We all knew full well that Bessie had never carried out a single accidental act in her entire life.

"He had been called out to the Castle Inn where a drink-fuelled argument looked as if it might get out of hand. The moment they saw my husband's six-foot-three frame, that's without his helmet, coming through the doorway, one of them downed his pint quickly and left. I recognised the name of the man who had stayed in the public bar – it was Billie Beynon. He's a farmer from Jameston who it seems rents a haybarn at the back of the Lamphey Road stables. He had accused the other drinker of taking more hay bales than he had paid for. It was only when I saw in the notebook that the departed party was none other than Shorty Stevens the hay merchant from Clarbeston Road that I realised that we have been coming towards this mystery from the wrong end. Shorty has come to my husband's attention a few times in the past, but has always proven that he was well away from any crime whenever or wherever it was committed."

Penny piped up. "At best then, if this Shorty has been up to no good, he's too clever to be caught. We'll have to let him know that we are on to him and send him packing."

Bessie concurred. "Too true girl, we need to expose his crime without showing our hand. I would like our two Night Owls, Auntie Sian and Glenys to stay behind. We will then agree on how to put paid to shifty Shorty and restore the Smithy's reputation."

∗∗∗

I couldn't wait another day to get the Night Owl's report, I'd persuaded Bron to let the four of us meet in the back room of the library on early closing Wednesday. She kindly offered us some homemade dandelion and burdock with ginger biscuits. Even though I am fond of a ginger, when Bron confirmed that the liquid refreshment had been made from a recipe in a borrowed book I enquired as to the borrower. The said brewer was well known to us and had left school without completing his education. It was not clear how far his skills in reading instructions had progressed since his early departure so we declined his homemade brew.

Glenys and I settled down to hear the report. Penny the Photo said that she had taken over Bron the Books' viewing point at the top of First Lane. Unlike her friend and fellow Night Owl, she wasn't reading a book but was wearing the toughest gardening gloves she could find. Bron, she explained was further down the lane in the next gateway and was armed with a powerful torch to be used the moment she saw any mounted figure or anything resembling one coming down the lane.

Penny continued. "Our patience was rewarded as the brisk clip-clop of hooves came into the lane just after midnight. I saw Bron leap out of the gateway. There was someone in dark clothing running alongside the large horse upon which a headless body had been mounted. Bron shouted at the top of her voice and waved her torch vigorously towards the apparition. The horse stopped in its tracks causing its guide to be pulled up short.

I came out of the gate and stepped silently up to the side of the horse. I pulled aside the canvas cover to reveal several bales of hay. I wrenched out a few large handfuls and tugged at the loosened twine holding the ghostly shape together. The hay bales collapsed and showered down onto the road. The guide dropped the reins, let out an unmanly scream and fled past me to the top of the lane before sprinting down towards the town.

Bron directed her torch down onto the road and walked up to the Shire taking its reins, the animal seemed to be happy enough to step through the piles of hay and be led over to the hedge to be tied to a branch.

I collected as much hay as I could hold and threw it over the opposite hedge into the back garden of the vicarage. Bron joined me and in next to no time we had transferred most of the hay-load evidence onto the church premises. We kept back an armful of hay each, collected the Shire and having made friends by means of a few carrots thoughtfully brought by Bron, the three of us made our way out of the lane and away from the town. We went across and up the

Lamphey road towards the stables. Not only did we tempt our captive beast with hay, but we also made sure there was plenty strewn up the verge.

***

My nephew was beaming, the queue had disappeared from the smithy. The bush telegraph across Pembroke had feverishly confirmed that a gang of international hay thieves had been interrupted in the middle of their illegal activities at the junction of First Lane and the Lamphey Road. Although no arrests had been made, it was reliably reported that the gang had retreated 'Up the Line'.

The alarm had been raised by the wife of the Vicar who had insisted that the police investigate a load of hay which had been showered upon her best sheets which had been left out overnight on the line to get a good blow. Sergeant Evans, who had taken on this investigation, had already pieced together clues which had arisen all over the town. A disagreement he attended to in the Castle Inn, a missing horseshoe which had been found some distance from the crime scene and finally a trail of hay from the vicarage leading back to the stables next to Farmer Beynon's haybarn had completed the picture for him.

I met Bessie the Law coming out of the butchers, she looked happy enough.

I asked her. "How are you now girl? Last I heard was that the Western Mail had interviewed your husband. Bit of a hero the article said."

Bessie put her hand on my arm and said, 'Auntie Sian, where would we be without my husband and his trusty notebook to keep the good people of Pembroke safe in their beds?"

We roared in laughter blocking the pavement then went over the road to Brown's café to share a Knickerbocker Glory.

The Kindness of Children – *Maggie the Shop*

I had just finished sewing three tablecloths together when Bessie the Law called the meeting of the Station Road Sewing Circle to order, ahead of conducting any other business. From table to floor, St Michael's church hall was covered in flags, bunting and lamp post decorations. Our leader had most likely decided that our handiwork, being created for the forthcoming Coronation street party, was up to or beyond the standards expected of our exclusive group. The tables were soon cleared and our creations were packed into a selection of large boxes ready for the big day, or to be more exact next Tuesday. It was time to get down to the serious business of keeping the town and its people safe.

Bessie stood and announced. "A very quiet week as far as we know ladies. The only incident in the town, I can report upon, was of a Dachshund and a German Shepherd carrying out a daring raid on the butcher's shop opposite the post office."

The newer members leaned forward to capture every detail of this unusual crime. Those of us who had been in the circle since its inception sat back and waited for Bessie's well-worn delivery to take place.

She continued. "The little dog jumped up, took a string of sausages from the counter and ran off up the main street towards the castle. The German shepherd apologised for his pet, saying that he was on holiday with his dog who had never taken an interest in sausages back at home. The butcher accepted the offered payment and said that it takes a good sausage dog to know a good sausage."

Bessie sat down. Her favourite yarn still made us laugh. I waited for her to start her round-robin of the twelve of us to see if anything untoward had happened since our last meeting. I was the only taker.

"In all my years serving people with their groceries, I've never come across such a strange encounter. A woman wearing red faded dungarees came into the shop this morning with her two young children. She spent ages looking for the cheapest food she could find. When I told her what was due, she pulled out a handful of small jewellery and offered it in payment. She pointed at each item, earrings, bracelets and small brooches, wanting me to pick the one I thought would be enough to settle her bill. The straps of her dungarees were frayed and the buckle on one side had been replaced by baling twine so I picked the smallest thing in her hand. My husband will have a fit when he comes to balance the till when we close tonight. In all the time we've had the shop I think it's the first time we've gone back to bartering. Then I noticed something odd about the children. They were about five and six years old, a boy and a girl. They were wearing identical tops which had been made from bright blue material with large yellow sunflowers on their shoulders. The stitching, done by hand, mind you, was beautiful, saying they were even and tidy wouldn't do them justice. Funny thing though, I've seen that pattern somewhere before, it'll come to me."

Bessie retorted. "I think you might be underestimating things there my girl!"

I smiled. "We all know what good stitching looks like Bessie, Lord knows, you've kept your eye on all of us as we've worked our pieces."

Bessie shook her head. "Not your needlework my love, I meant the ages of the children, I'm sure I saw the same woman wearing red dungarees coming out of the public toilets about dinner time with two girls about eight and nine, they were wearing orange striped blouses with puff shoulders and navy-blue shorts – very smart. I'd say though, they were nearer eight and nine years old."

Maria from Milan seemed to be more interested in the woman than her clothes. "Did she speak at all, perhaps to her children?" She looked at me for an answer.

"Not to them, they were well behaved, but as she left, she said 'Diolch yn fawr' She must think that we speak Welsh here."

Maria tilted her chin. "Seems like I'm not the only one from a faraway place."

Bessie said. "I hope we have another chance to meet her, she needs to know that we're a friendly crowd, not to mention that she's a tidy seamstress. In the meantime, we've a lot to do before next Tuesday. These street decorations must be finished and put up the length of Station Road. It's once in a lifetime we all get to celebrate having a new Queen, so we'd better make the best of it."

***

Joan the Tip, her husband drove the dustbin lorry, was at the top of a step-ladder tying bunting onto a lamppost in Station Road. She had no trouble with heights, often saying that after producing four children in as many years there wasn't much left in life to be worried about. I had pulled the line of triangular flags taut and secured it across this side of the road when the woman in the red dungarees and two older girls walked underneath it. I called to Joan and pointed, she turned to look, shook her head and clung on to the lamppost. She descended and came over to me, gasping "Did you see that? I nearly fainted for the first time in my entire life."

I put my hand on her shoulder. "You've gone as pale as the tablecloths I've been sewing together for the party."

Joan was still shaking. "That's exactly it, did you see what those girls were wearing?"

"Appliqued skirts if I remember rightly," I observed, "very ornate pattern too. They suited the girls who must have been at least eleven or twelve,"

Joan had regained her breath. "The mystery is indeed mounting over how many children Mrs Red Dungarees has but what shook me to my core was that they were both wearing skirts which had the same embroidered pattern as the tablecloth which Mrs Govan-Price, you know I do a bit of cleaning for her, had brought me back from Austria. Now that is what I call a coincidence too far."

I picked up the end of another length of bunting. "It would seem, that she has six children up to now, who are all wearing well-made garments. It came to me last night where I'd seen the yellow sunflowers on the youngest children's tops. It's the same pattern as

Megan the Signals' front room curtains."

Joan replied. "Wouldn't surprise me if the material for the orange striped blouses that the middle children were wearing had come from somewhere in town. Although I can't see how they could possibly have entered our homes."

I had secured the next decoration. "Before we get carried away and make a mountain out of a mystery, I think we ought to let Bessie know what we've learned. Now, we'd better get on with the rest of the lampposts; by the way, did you find someone with a television?"

Joan smiled. "Mrs Foreman the sweetshop has bought one and put it in her back parlour. She invited a couple of us regulars and our families in. Mind you, it's on the strict understanding that none of our children will be allowed to go anywhere near the shop without an adult present."

I picked up my ladder and moved on. "We'll be watching the coronation with Carol from Chapel, the elders and a few families. It's only rented, Carol wanted to buy one but one of the elders was against it. His wife finally convinced him that not all progress at the BBC is the work of the devil and that television will eventually have a place in our society. What really changed his mind though, was when she pointed out that Her Majesty wouldn't enjoy her special day if she knew that one of her most loyal subjects had decided to look the other way."

***

The full creative powers of the Station Road Sewing Circle were being employed. Megan the Signals and me were stitching the final straps onto a tall tubular structure with a cone on the top. It was covered in a metallic silver material with holes for the wearer's arms and legs. At the base of the tube which it must be said, tended to make the wearer bandy, there were two smaller holes on opposite sides to represent the eye of the needle. Megan's youngest daughter, skinny as a rake so to speak, was taking no notice of her mother's constant requests to stand still.

To the right of us, Joan the Tip and Bessie the Law were putting the finishing touches on the round tub of cardboard being worn by

Joan's youngest. The circular top through which his head emerged had been embroidered with the name of a well-known haberdashery. The sides which had holes for his arms had been painstakingly wrapped and stitched with spare clotheslines to represent the thread normally to be found on a cotton reel.

On the other side of the hall Carol from Chapel and Maria from Milan had taken a similar contraption off Carol's daughter who had made it plain that now that it had been confirmed that she could get into it, she would prefer to go down the park to play. The diameter of the base was slightly larger than at the top which was domed and allowed for the wearer's head to come through. They were carefully making indents all over the entire surface of the metallic paper which had been glued to the structure. Carol said that anyone who had picked up a sewing pattern would know immediately that the object before them was indeed a thimble. I was happy that our entries for the fancy dress competition would certainly gain attention if not a single prize.

When all three exhibits had been brought up to Bessie's level of approval, the remaining children were released and the kettle was put on.

Bessie called the meeting to order. "As originally reported by Maggie the shop, our new neighbours, a family of increasing proportions it seems, are becoming the kind of mystery, which no self-respecting sewing circle can allow to go on."

She turned to Joan. "I understand that you have investigated the appearance of an Austrian embroidered pattern on the skirts that the two eldest children were wearing?"

Joan leaned forward. "I certainly have, my tablecloth is missing from the airing cupboard but I haven't made any enquiries indoors or out until we've had this meeting."

Bessie nodded; she was more than satisfied with Joan's efforts.

"Megan, when Maggie told you about the children's sunflower tops, you had a good look around your cottage?"

"I certainly did; I went straight home to discover that my spare set of curtains for the front room have disappeared. Same as Joan I've not told a soul."

Carol chipped in. "It was all I could do to keep this to myself when we first came into the church hall today, two of my best pillowcases, orange striped they are, have vanished off the face of the earth. Well now that's not entirely true, I'm sure they have been reincarnated as a pair of tops for two of the children in our visiting family."

Joan said. "It's looking black for them isn't it, I think it's time to pay them a visit."

Carol agreed. "That's the next step surely but we don't know where they are living."

Bessie summarised. "We haven't got all the facts at our fingertips, even if we knew where they were, we couldn't just barge in and accuse the family of anything."

I spoke up. "I've had limited dealings with the family, perhaps I should go to see them. At least I'm not a complete stranger. Can I suggest that we all keep a lookout for them. If someone could tip me off that they were in town, I would propose that I follow them home and get their side of the story."

Bessie concurred. "You are so right Maggie. one word of caution, it's best if all this is kept to ourselves until the full picture emerges."

***

I had barely come in and put on my shop overall when the telephone rang. It was Bessie. "Reported sighting on the commons. Operation Stitch in Time is live. Suggest you intercept on Station Road Square."

Bessie had worked in the Ministry of Information during the war. Her legendary vocabulary in an eighteen-word telegram had built her reputation for delivering the news, good or bad, but nothing but the news.

I took my coat from the hallstand and walked briskly up the main street.

I'd been looking at the display of fruit and vegetables that adorned the front of Sidney William's shop on the square for a few minutes when the two girls wearing the most decorative aspects of Joan's tablecloth came up the Gooses Lane and walked up Station Road. They were chattering. I picked up a few phrases and was surprised to learn that my intended targets were speaking English interspersed with what I assumed was Welsh. I was grateful that they were oblivious to their surroundings and more to the point my being in hot pursuit. The three of us had left the town behind, passed the Smithy and the entrance to First Lane when the girls disappeared into a field. I hurried to see where they had gone. I turned into the gateway and stopped. There were five children playing in the field. I recognised some of them. The girl was Megan the Signals' middle child and the boy was Joan the Tip's youngest. In one corner of the field, there was a work-weary shepherd's hut on wheels. Smoke was coming out of the battered chimney and voices spilt out from within. The girls went up the steps and entered. I walked across the freshly mown grass, went up the steps, tapped on the side of the open door and said. "Good afternoon, my name is Maggie, can I compliment you on your dressmaking and needlework?

**

We had all watched the crowning of our Queen go off without a hitch. We were mesmerised, to say the least, to see on the small screen, Her Majesty walking across the corner of the chapel assembly room. The children had shown great interest at first, but in small numbers they had left the proceedings. The others would be thinking it most likely that the youngsters would be making their way to Station Road to survey the long line of tables laid out up the centre of the street and deduce which end would be most likely to carry the most food. As it happened, I knew differently.

Not all of the children sat in their chosen seats as the adults emerged from both sides of the street loaded down with enough food to feed the first regiment of the Royal Welsh Fusiliers.

I couldn't help looking up the Lamphey road every minute, towards the latest addition to our celebrations. Bessie was the first to see the little army coming down the road. To be exact there were eight of our children coming away from the Apostolic church carrying its famous and feared folding chairs. When erected every one inclined downwards to the front which caused the seated person to hang on for dear life. It had never been established if this was a manufacturing fault or whether Miss Jenkins, the Supervisor, a leading light in the church, mind you, had requested the feature to prevent people from nodding off during her sometimes-lengthy sermons.

Behind the chair bearers were the older children carrying a long table top. Bringing up the rear of this unusual, you might say Coronation cavalcade, were several children each holding a trestle support. Maria, who was the only other person I had drawn into my plan emerged from the church and directed the children to set up the table and chairs as an extension of the existing arrangement. She produced two sheets out of a bag and covered the bare wood to match the rapidly filling tables. I wondered if anyone else would be sleeping on a bare mattress on Coronation night. The children stepped back to reveal a second procession coming down from the Lamphey Road. The entire street, still holding sandwiches, cakes, jellies, trifles and countless tea-time treats watched as a couple, she in red dungarees and he wearing a threadbare suit were followed by their six children. They walked in pairs and approached the newly assembled table where Maria spoke briefly to them with a big smile on her face. They stood a little awkwardly behind their nominated chairs and waited. The street party sprung into life. The time for an explanation I had decided would be later. Appetites were more than ready to be satisfied. The tables groaned under the weight of the feast now running up the entire length of the tables. I moved swiftly amongst the previous owners of the sunflower tops, striped blouses and embroidered skirts to assure them that all would be explained as soon as the party was finished, the tables cleared to one side and the games had started. I was becoming hopeful that all concerned knew by now this was going to be a story well worth waiting for.

***

The fancy dress competition had been won by a five-year-old girl, not that her two-tone crepe paper gown and cardboard crown had been a work of art. In the right light, from the side that is, she looked very much like the Queen. I thought that her future was well-assured through an ongoing appearance on all subsequent coins of the realm. No one in the sewing circle who had slaved over the needle, cotton reel or thimble outfits was unduly concerned, as Beryl the Will put it, you can't argue with good looks and not everyone in life will end up

77

having their face on a sixpence.

We sat against the front wall of Joan the Tip's house and were enjoying a long-awaited cup of tea and they were making it plain to me that the time for a full explanation had arrived.

I announced. "I'll start at the beginning and go on from there. Mr and Mrs Roberts are from Blaenau Ffestiniog. He is a skilled farm labourer who has moved to Pembrokeshire to gain promotion to Dairy-man at a farm in Stackpole. They came down ready to move into their large tied cottage last week only to find the current occupant still there, his move to a Farm Manager's job in Cheltenham won't now happen until July. Now here's the thing, the family only brought enough clothes for a few days; the rest of their possessions are packed and still in Blaenau." I paused to look at my line of friends, all eyes were unwaveringly upon me.

I gave a slight cough to herald a gear change in my story. "They were offered the use of the shepherd's hut because their previous home was by now occupied. They had no choice but to move in. The children had already made friends down the park and had been invited by our children to the street party. When the Roberts' children said 'no thank you' because all they had to wear were the clothes they were stood in, our Station Road youngsters went into action. They looked for items at home which had never been used to their memory and gave them to Mrs Roberts. As we now know she is an accomplished seamstress and produced the clothes which were the first thing that we noticed when they came into town. Joan, Megan and Carol sat back; I could see from their expressions that pride had overtaken any thought of punishment for the donations made without parental approval.

I added. "Mrs Roberts was mortified when she found out the items had been taken without your permission. However, I can see on your faces, you are reaping the benefits now, of how you've brought your children up.

Joan said. "They must be down to their last pennies if Mrs Roberts is paying her way with small baubles."

I looked over at the couple who were deep in conversation with Maria's husband Antonio the Milk. "They could do with a helping hand until their cottage becomes free. Maria, will you go over to

78

Georgie Rossiter at the farm tomorrow morning and offer him an extra pair of hands to get the harvest in. Beryl, would you check at the Town hall through your husband if there are any council houses empty for the next few weeks. I'm sure we can all hunt out material for Mrs Roberts to make her family a few more clothes. If it was to her liking, we could welcome her as a temporary member of our sewing circle before she moves out to Stackpole. This is one occasion I would say when our acts of kindness need to follow the good examples set by the Station Road children."

The Right Pegs – *Beryl the Will*

With all the modesty I could call upon I shared my quilting prowess with the other members of the Station Road Sewing Circle. As the wife of the Town Clerk and Pembroke's foremost solicitor, I had kept my reputation for brevity while revealing the log cabin design which adorned my latest project. The main reason, however, for getting on with it was my prior announcement that I would be seeking the Sewing Circle's assistance to resolve my husband's dilemma. I could see that tea was being daintily gulped down and larger portions than usual of cake were being consumed within each mouthful.

I set out the facts of the puzzling matter. "My husband in his position as Town Clerk has been going through the personal application forms for the post of Borough Transport manager. Dewi Moffatt has just retired. The field has been narrowed down to three candidates and the Council is expecting him to present his preferred applicant along with justifications. He can't get past these last three. I've had whole nights of sighing and I've even missed three radio episodes of 'A book at bedtime,' when he's brought the files to bed to see if he can draw any further conclusions aided by his cocoa."

Megan the Signals was supportive. "Surely, he's done this before with other Council vacancies, what's the difference this time? He can't be harking back to the funny business with the park-keeper, can he?"

"You've hit the nail on the head girl," I concurred. "How was my husband to know that the man ran a flower stall in Haverfordwest market? The park had been almost stripped of all flower beds by the time the criminal was caught red-handed with two dozen rose shrubs selling them door to door in Fishguard. My husband needs to get this one right"

Bessie the Law wanted me to move on. "To give your husband his fair dues, the three applicants must all be good people if he can't find a favourite, but we are missing a few things here, are they locals and are they married?" she looked at me. "I'm assuming that you've caught a brief glimpse of what's in their files!"

"None of them is local," I affirmed, "without him knowing I've seen that they all have families and they come from London, Newport Mon and Edinburgh respectively."

Maggie the Shop was excited. "Apart from sounding like an old joke, an Englishman, a Welshman and so on, this is starting to shape up to at least a couple of interview teas; we've done a few of those in our time."

I lifted my hand. "My lights have come on again; I'll suggest that he can't make any sound recommendations with an open mind until after he's interviewed all three. I'll then add that it's a pity the wives couldn't see how nice Pembroke is, that said their opinions might cause one or more of the candidates to drop out. That'll persuade him. However, we know from experience that the three wives will want to see where they might be moving to. We can offer them a tour and keep the ladies separate as we walk them around the town then we'll conduct our interviews over a cup of Welsh tea and a friendly chat."

Bessie the Law had been making notes. "Glenys and Joan could be in Brown's café, Megan and Carol can do the Cromwell tea rooms, and I and Bronwen will have our tea in the backroom in the King's Arms."

I was delighted. "Let's get this recruitment ball of ours rolling without my husband being any the wiser."

Bessie was smiling. "With due respect to your husband Beryl, Town Clerk or not, keeping our men in the dark is essential for us to spread our light and goodwill all over the town." The sound of chairs being pushed back and then stacked against the wall conveyed to all of us that the Station Road Sewing Circle was once again setting out on a mission.

***

It was the fourth time that my husband had read the same article in Golfing Monthly, 'How to improve your handicap without lifting a club.' I knew that his mind wasn't on it by the glance he gave, more than once, at the three files which had been sitting on the sideboard for days.

I settled into my armchair complete with knitting. "It'll be a good job done when you've recruited the right man into Dewi's job!" I ventured.

"I wish that was the end of it." He sighed. "As it is I can't see any bit of daylight between those three," he waved at the files, "not to mention there are more council employees nearing retirement so I'll be going through all of this pandemonium, right through to the end of the year."

I had achieved the first step in taking my husband to the starting point of our sewing circle's mission; making him trudge through his own self-misery.

"Two of them might turn the job down after you've taken them around the depot in Pembroke Dock! You've said yourself that Dewi was the captain of his own chaos down there."

He shook his head. "They are too keen to be put off, I'll just have to hope that they give me something to work on when I interview them next week."

"Be fair to yourself," I offered. "If any of them are family men you'll have no control over what they go back and say to their wives."

He sighed. "As it happens, they all are married with children, but I can't see how that helps me."

I didn't bat an eyelid. I couldn't have written a better script for my husband,

"The men won't have seen much around the town," I pointed out. "between having a taxi from the station, being in your office and going down to the depot at the bottom of Ferry Lane. Their wives will want to know where the schools are, the doctor's surgery, the chemist and the shops. It'll be guesswork built up with impressions by the time the men travel back home. What if all the wives put their feet down? You'll end up without a single candidate."

The golfing magazine had been put on the carpet.

"My only option then, to keep this on the rails is to ask them to bring their wives to see for themselves."

"That isn't a bad idea at all." I concurred and waited.

"I suppose I could get one of the girls in the office to show them around, or would it need three to keep them apart, wouldn't want any embarrassing encounters, would we?"

I was still waiting.

"Then again, I can't afford to have my staff tied up in this all day. This is becoming a bigger headache than selecting the right candidate."

He had slumped back into his chair.

I put down my knitting. "I thought your idea was good, shame to not see it working. If all you need to solve all of this is a few people to guide the wives around the town, why don't I ask my sewing circle if they can help out?"

He brightened up. "You would all know where everything is," He cleared his throat, "your help in making my idea work is much appreciated."

I was on the home stretch now. "What if we treat them to a nice Welsh tea to round off their visit, there are enough places to choose from in town."

My husband picked up his magazine and thumbed through to his place.

"That's settled then, Dewi's replacement will be in the bag by the end of next week."

***

I stepped into the library, which could only be described as full to the rafters. To be more precise there were six women including Bronwen spread around the shelves indicating that their interests ranged from 'Romantic cruises down the river Nile' to 'Classical music for those who just don't care.' The moment the town clock struck five o'clock and Bronwen locked up, the true purpose of our gathering emerged. We found enough chairs and cups and saucers to warrant putting the kettle on and formally open the follow-up meeting of Operation Right Pegs.

Responding to my invitation, Joan related what had gone on in

Brown's café. "For a slight girl, Vicky had a decent appetite I thought when she polished off her seventh Welsh cake. Our Bara-Brith loaf had been well-dented and the three of us were on our second pot of tea before we learned much. She told us that she and Dave her husband, were desperate to leave London, even though many people would love to live in their capital city. Vicky had an easy smile about her and was honest with us, she confessed that she did like having all the department stores at hand but her home isn't all that big so everywhere seems to be topped up with purchases, not to mention shoes, she'd bought up the West End. She is looking for a place where things could be a bit tidier for Dave, he often says to her 'you can only wear one pair of shoes at a time, the rest are simply showing off.' We certainly have the same views on bringing up a family. Vicky said it was spend spend spend all the time and that the streets and pavements of London are built to last, unlike her children's footwear. When Glenys said Vicky wouldn't know she had children down here, they'd be up Holyland woods or out at Freshwater East beach and all they need is money for pop and crisps Vicky said she'd save her husband a small fortune."

Without a moment's delay, Glenys picked up where Joan had left off,

"I said to her, money has been a bit tight then? Vicky replied that's what attracted Dave to the job, he's always on the lookout for better wages or lower outgoings. I asked her if Dave had had a tough upbringing, and she said that he had joined a boxing club when he was thirteen, as a way to stay out of trouble. Never been on the wrong side of the law to this day.

Joan asked if he would be bringing some of his boxing skills with him, you know, as if he is still on his toes, so to speak. Vicky said he certainly would and that she hoped he'd get the job. Pembroke would be a lovely place to bring her family up."

Glenys then glanced at Joan; the look said it all. I sensed that their summary was on its way. Glenys made her report. "Dave is a bit of a city boy but he has plenty of go in him. He would keep the workforce in the depot on their toes too. Joan and I think he is a front-runner. His wife is keen on coming to Pembroke because she'll be able to be thrifty and would love to run a tidier if not larger household."

We put the kettle on again before we heard from Megan and Carol. Conducting interviews and putting things to right was clearly thirsty work.

Megan was enthusiastic. "Eira from Newport Mon, loved history. She was obsessed with walking in the steps of the great, going by what she told us. When we'd stopped outside the Cromwell tea rooms and I had explained that it was from that very spot in 1648 that Oliver Cromwell had set siege to Pembroke castle, we thought she was going to faint with excitement. I did add that whilst there was no record of him stopping there for tea, there was plenty of evidence to show that Margaret Beaufort had given birth to Henry the Seventh in the castle. She had most likely wheeled him around Pembroke in his pram to get some fresh air into him on more than one occasion.

We enjoyed the tea-rooms speciality, cream along with jam on our Welsh cakes. Eira asked us if it was an English custom brought here by Oliver Cromwell when Carol said it was a possibility the girl was beside herself. 'He is so different to me, he never looks back' she told me when I asked her what drives her husband. "That's my Mike's motto, he is always looking to the future. Whenever we go on holiday, he plans it right down to towels for laying on the sand and others for drying yourself."

Carol took over,

"I said to her that her husband will get plenty of holidays to plan for if he worked for the Council. Right through the summer, all of them could be out on any of the beaches around here, some are only a bike ride away. Eira said it was strange that I should mention that because they all have bikes. She explained that although they would like to ride more there wasn't much room to ride around the back streets of Newport. The coal trains coming through from the valleys down to the docks left their trail of coal dust everywhere. She even said that the best time to put her washing out was overnight when the trains are not running. I made her smile when I said, 'And there's us complaining when the fresh sea breezes blow our sheets into next door.'

Megan took up the report once more. "I asked Eira if her husband had always been keen on planning then? She told us a family story about him when he was a boy; he would copy down the programmes from the Radio Times to decide what to listen to on his old cat's whiskers radio set in his bedroom. Trouble was, that by the time he finished his list, the first two programmes had already been transmitted. We smiled to let her know that boys and men can be funny sometimes."

Carol turned to me to round off their report. "I hope very much that this information will help your husband select the right man for the job. We liked Eira, she might be excited about the past but it was plain to us that her Mike was a man with his eyes firmly set on the future."

Bessie asked her. "What's the verdict then?"

Carol replied. "Mike is a sensible Welshman for sure. He needs to know what is coming over the mountain, so to speak, because he wants to be ready for it. Eira wants to leave behind the history of Welsh coal and the mess it leaves. It's a pity we are trying to fit three pegs into a single hole."

Bearing in mind that Bronwen had been hopping up and down keeping our teacups full it didn't surprise me when Bessie gave their report,

Me and Bronwen had wondered if we would understand anything that Aileen might say, her being from the city of Edinburgh. However, our fears were dispelled the moment she greeted us and confirmed that she had been brought up in southern Liverpool by Scottish parents. She said that she was more than comfortable with the Welsh accent due to the many migrants coming up to the city from North Wales to find work. The Welsh afternoon tea was going down nicely, the cake plate never went down below half full. The staff at the Kings Arms public house wanted to show our visitors that there was more to their customer service than pulling a pint.

Aileen confirmed to us that her husband Rab was the one with Gaelic roots, she explained that he came down to work briefly in Liverpool, they met and married but for most of their lives, they've lived in and around Edinburgh. I said that it'll be a bit of a wrench for you to leave such a beautiful city, coming down here to a rural Welsh town and all. She agreed, saying that she loved everything about the Scottish capital. The military tattoo, festivals, the shows, libraries and museums but then said all that means little if your man isn't happy in his work."

Bronwen asked her why he works there if he doesn't like his job. She explained that when they came back up from Liverpool, the workforce was still closely knit then. They were all on first-name terms with anyone the moment they walked in the door. I remarked that it didn't sound like a bad place to work, what turned things around?"

Aileen looked a bit upset then; I wondered if we had gone too far. She pulled herself together and said a couple of years ago the firm was bought out by a big company, that brought in some so-called business efficiency people. She said from what Rab had told her these so-called experts walked around with stop-watches, telling people that they should work harder and not to lean on the loyalty they'd given in previous years."

When Bronwen asked her if that was why they'd come down to Pembroke to find a life that isn't chasing quality this and quality that? Aileen said that if Rab wasn't at his interview, he'd tell us about his first job. Every single bit of his work was scrutinised by an older employee. The old man found loads wrong with Rab's work but he never went on about the errors only how the bad workmanship, if possible, could be repaired and later how it could be avoided. Before Rab became a manager, he was the union representative. He rescued the company and his workmates from more than one strike by looking for common interests and not dwelling on their differences. She sighed and said she was sure he would be much happier here and that he'd seek out every opportunity to help those who are struggling in a job for which they've never been properly trained."

Bessie stopped to let us take it all in.

I said. "So where do we stand on Rab then?"

Bessie pulled out two slips of paper. She read from the first one. "Bronwen and I agreed that Rab is a real man with a heart and a half inside him. He sees the best in people even when they might be disappointing him. He doesn't believe in dropping others in at the deep end. He's coming to Pembroke to carry on practising his important values. However, he would probably draw the line at supporting our national rugby team."

She paused again, this time, to allow us to separate fact from

87

fiction.

We all expected no less than a full report from Bessie, if she hadn't been a policeman's wife, she would have been a headmistress.

Bessie wasn't finished. "His wife puts his ambitions before her own and that is why she would be prepared to move from Scotland right across the country to West Wales. She is a woman who is ready to give up all that a capital city can offer to bring up her family with a happy father."

She picked up the other slip. "My other enquiries based on the considerable flow of information moving across the town every morning over cups of tea, garden fences and accidentally overheard conversations, have revealed that there are four more retirements due of council managers this year, they are: Canteen and Food Supplies, Planning and Building Controls, Highway Repairs and Personnel."

Glenys responded. "Before we go down this list can we agree that Dave from London is indeed the best candidate for the new Transport Manager?" The others assented with a wave of their hands.

Bessie glanced at the library clock, which had moved on without pausing for breath,

"We will have to see what we can do for the other two excellent but unsuccessful candidates" she urged us, "we will need to have a chat, on the side of course, with the appropriate wives of the pending retirees. This approach has worked for us before, we need to convince the wives that having their husbands retire earlier would be the best for all concerned." The town hall clock above the library struck six reminding most of us that we still had to put an evening meal in front of our families.

***

"In the golfing vernacular," announced my husband from his armchair. "I played a hole-in-one today in front of the whole Town Council. Everyone in the chamber wanted to shake my hand."

He waited to receive even more praise from me. I was smiling. "I am so pleased, after all your hard work over these last months you thoroughly deserve it."

"Can't say it was all down to me", his false modesty was well meant. "I have had several helping hands."

I placed my knitting on the carpet and folded my hands neatly in my lap. "Who might these helping angels be then?"

My glowing husband revealed. "I wouldn't call them angels but they certainly brought me good news. Jimmy Barrett from Planning and Building Controls popped in to see me a few days ago. He said, out of the blue, mind you, that if I could see my way to get him an allotment at the back of Woodbine Terrace, he'd be happy to take his retirement early. I said it would only take a telephone call to the Parks and Gardens department."

I gave a small frown. "Isn't that another headache for you? More recruitment?"

"There's a lot more to this, let me go on. Barry the People, do you know I can't think of his last name in all this excitement, you know him, the Personnel manager was in the Kings Arms after work having a half. I popped in to settle the bill for the tea party that your sewing circle had kindly given for the interviewees' wives when he called me over. He wanted to give me fair warning that he wouldn't be retiring at all unless I could find him the exceptional person capable of looking after his flock. Barry is a lay preacher with the Baptist Church you know, always on the lookout for lost sheep or lost causes for that matter."

My husband paused to allow me time for me to absorb his not-so-surprising revelations.

He continued. "I told him that anyone coming into his job could have a three months handover which would give him plenty of time to show the new boy the ropes!

He sat back in triumph.

I wanted him to enjoy his moment a little more. "Please carry on, I've a feeling the real master stroke in all this, excuse any reference to golf, has yet to be revealed."

He stood up and walked around the room, he was striding the corridors of success. "I had already decided that Dave was best suited to the Transport job, they need more than a shake-up down there. I had pulled out the files on Mike and Rab and was about to write, with care I might add, their rejection letters. That's when I came to my senses. I had here two excellent candidates and if I could allow Barry the People this extended handover and secure that allotment for Jimmy Barrett, I could solve three problems, not one. Rab could go into Personnel and Mike would do a good job in Planning and Building Controls. I'd already told Dave that he had been successful, I rang Mike and Rab, and they accepted my respective offers on the spot."

I hadn't seen that big smile on my husband's face since he had won the golfing cup for 'Best new member using borrowed clubs.'

I beamed. "What can I say? Well done, boy!"

"Sorry for what I've put you through, you've been a rock. I couldn't have done it all without you behind me."

I thought – Not to mention selected members of the Station Road Sewing Circle.

***

I came in the door of St Michael's church hall to see that Bessie was already setting out the chairs. The main item on any other business agenda was to celebrate the successful recruitment of three new council managers with yet again, more tea and plenty of cake.

"Could we clear up a slight gap in the tactics you used to give my husband his solution?"

She responded by pulling two chairs together. "I thought you might be early today due to our slight change of plan."

I sat down and put my hand on my friend's arm. "When I first learned from my husband that Barry the People had no intention of retiring, I thought we had come unstuck. The lovely Scotsman would be staying north of the border."

Bessie smiled. "That was my first reaction when I bumped into Barry's wife and we went into Brown's café for a cup of tea." I caught the accidental inference but I knew that Bessie had set out that morning with the sole intent of hunting Barry's wife down.

Bessie continued. "She wanted him to retire before he has to, his legs play him up a bit. He was adamant that he wasn't prepared to let his working relationship with every council employee be ruined by some new-fangled stranger. I talked it through with her and we realised that we needed to use a different approach. We finally agreed that she would say that she supported her husband's decision to work, but if the Town Clerk found, by divine intervention, a suitable replacement, it would only be fair to give the man a chance. Better still Barry would have the final say on it all.

I nodded and cut in. "We knew from Rab's wife that he would be singing off the same song sheet as Barry. Wouldn't be surprised if they ended up as a duet."

Bessie was happy now that it was all cleared up. She stood up and finished setting out the chairs.

I went into the kitchen to sort out the cups and saucers, I wondered if Jimmy Barrett had been down to his allotment yet.

The Black Diamonds – *Glenys the Coal*

Bessie the Law stood up with that resigned look on her, which she usually reserved for fair to middling news, she then told us,

"They have been released early from their detention at her Majesty's pleasure and as I speak, they are travelling by train from Swansea to Pembroke. Notwithstanding the distance from Swansea jail to the railway station, we can expect a crime wave to commence around seven this evening. Yes ladies, Dai and Dafydd the naughty boys who never grew up are back amongst us."

We ladies, that is the members of the Station Road Sewing Circle, broke out, to a woman, into broad smiles.

Bessie continued over our slight murmurs. "I know their antics make us smile more than cry but we still must keep our eyes on them. The last thing we want is for those two to be in the middle of one of their crooked schemes when the Welcome to West Wales judges are paying us one of their surprise visits. So, let's be on a full alert from this evening if you please."

The tea and cakes were then served. I was about to make good use of a huge rock cake, many of the contributing cooks in our Circle never bothered with measures, when Maria from Milan sat down next to me complete with her tea and scone.

"Glenys girl, who are Dai and Dafydd? She asked me. "I wasn't a member of the Sewing Circle when they went to prison, I wondered if you could put me in the picture?"

I nodded, she had come to the right person, it was myself and two other members who had worked hard to keep the Thomas boys out of jail but our efforts had been in vain.

"Best if I tell you why they were put away last time. They were selling one-foot square pieces of turf which carried a certificate which assured the buyer that it was the very same grass from inside Pembroke castle as in 1648 when Oliver Cromwell broke the siege and entered the stronghold in triumph."

Maria asked me. "Were you involved in their arrest?"

"Not directly, as you know we work in secret. One of our members had an elderly relation who played bowls in Pembroke Dock. He mentioned in passing that their warm-up green was getting smaller every few nights, it would be only a couple of weeks before they would be warming up on a postage stamp. A lot of enquiries across the town led us to Dai and Dafydd but before we could put things back to where they had been, they were apprehended."

Maria rubbed her brow. "I thought that Dai and Dafydd are versions of the same English name. Aren't they both David?

I smiled. "It's another story but it's worth telling you now. There's one year between the two young men. The older boy is John David Thomas. When the registrar came around the maternity ward to register the birth of her second child, Mrs Thomas thought he'd asked her the name of her previous boy. She said 'John David', but the registrar said you can't have the same name twice, so she was still drowsy from the gas and said 'Sorry, I meant David John'. All went well until the older boy was eight years old and he decided he liked the name David for himself. Because they were a handful at that age, she gave in and renamed them Dai and Dafydd. Dai is bright and comes up with all their ill-fated money-making schemes and Dafydd provides the muscle."

Maria shook her head. "I think I've kept up with all of that, is there a Mr Thomas?"

I picked up my cup and saucer. "The boys were still sharing a pram when he was last seen catching the ferry across the Cleddau and heading up into the north of the county."

Maria sat back. "That makes sense now. We are intent on keeping people safe in their beds, that's why we will do all we can to save the grown-up naughty boys from themselves."

***

Since the last time we were in St Michael's church hall, much to my surprise, things had been quiet. Bessie had sent a message to us all to stand down from the alert condition to normal eyes and ears picking up snippets and placing them on the grapevine. However, I didn't share the others' relief because I was fuming. Bessie could see that I was livid.

She stood up. "Ladies I think we should make some time for Glenys the Coal here, it seems to me that she needs to share her feelings."

I gave Bessie a nod, I was ready to give the girls the full works,

"I have always made it my business to regularly call in on my husband's important customers to make sure that they were entirely happy with his coal delivery service. The mandatory cup of tea also provided the time needed for me to extract any newsworthy items for passing on to my sister members in this room. If there was any bother from the coal lorry parking on the pavement and sending young mothers with prams out into the busy road, I would have a quiet word with the driver. Should there be any stray lumps of coal indoors, falling from any bag as they were being carried out the back, I would remind the coalmen that the merchandise would only be paid for when the entire delivery reached the coal bunker. Truth be told there were very few incidents. However, this latest complaint which has been rigorously lodged by Mrs Hughes on the East Back has upset me, to say the least. 'Your Nantgarw Bright is second to none Glenys,' Mrs Hughes often has said to me nicely: so she stopped me in my tracks when she said, 'Up to now that is."

I waited for the expectancy in the room to go up a notch. "Mrs Hughes then annoyed me further by saying that she didn't mind picking up the odd pieces that fell on her best Persian hall carpet as the coalman comes through the house, because she liked to keep the side gate secured for her safety and the anyway the lock is rusted up."

I didn't even start to defend myself because I knew there was more. She always liked to make a mystery out of a molehill. She then said that much to her surprise on the delivery before last, not a single piece of coal fell out, not even a bit of slack mind you. It was the same as the previous week. I thought that was it but before I could open my mouth, she launched her wicked accusation. She poured it out, saying that she had made a point of standing on the stairs, looking in the bag as the coalman passed her and saw that the level of the coal was a couple of inches below the top of the sacks, that's why there hadn't been a single spillage!"

I raised my hands in exasperation, everyone around the room was waiting to hear how I had defended my husband.

"I gave it to her good and proper. If you are inferring that you have been given short measure Mrs Hughes, I told her, I can assure you that every bag of Nantgarw Bright that comes into your home has been measured to the nearest lump on our scales back at the Pembroke station coal yard. There was nothing more I could say except - Well now, I won't be putting anything to rights if I stop for idle chat, I'll be on my way to sort this out once and for all, don't you worry Mrs Hughes. Her face was a picture, standing there with the tea strainer in her hand, I can tell you; I even saw myself out."

***

Having shared most of the story so far, I looked around the Sewing Circle. All eyes were upon me, determined not to miss a clue, I didn't disappoint them,

"Now – here is the mystery I went into the coal yard very early today and checked the bags on the lorry delivering to Mrs Hughes. They load up the night before and as she is their first drop, her bag of coal was stacked on the very back of the lorry. It was the only one which wasn't filled to the brim. So, I'm in a quandary now, as to whether this is someone who has got it in for Mrs Hughes or indeed my husband's business."

"What did you do? asked Bessie.

"What could I do, I picked up a shovel and filled the bag up! I'm not having another mouthful of Earl Grey with Mrs Hughes until we solve this one."

Penny the Photo observed. "Are you saying that when the bag went on the scales the previous day it was the same weight as the others even though it wasn't full?"

I shook my head. "I can confirm it must have weighed the same. the lorry gets weighed before it leaves the coal yard but I couldn't say for sure whether Mrs Hughes's bag was full or not."

Penny was more than interested. "If we say the coalman had filled the bag and then weighed it, he would know that it wasn't full to the top. Don't you think the change in level has occurred overnight.?"

I had to agree. "I suppose we could say that, but why only Mrs Hughes's bag?

Bron the Books chipped in. "If someone is interfering with the bag overnight it could be more due to where the bag is on the lorry than who it is intended for."

Penny was up and running by now. "Too right Bron, I think this is a job for one of us Night Owls."

Bessie smiled at our youngest members of the sewing circle, Penny, and Bron both went to bed very late. On several occasions, one of their nightly vigils had more than helped our Sewing Circle to solve a mystery.

"We need to see who is behind all this," Bessie summarised looking at Penny then me, "without, of course, letting anyone know of our involvement. I suggest that our first Night Owl excursion will be conducted by Penny, assisted by Glenys who knows her way around the coal yard. It will have to be the night before the next delivery to Mrs Hughes."

She said to me. "If you don't mind filling up her bags before they go out for delivery until we solve this at least, then your husband's reputation will remain intact and more to the point we will intentionally stay out of the spotlight."

***

I was the first to make my report to the sewing circle. Since I had been topping up Mrs Hughes's coal bags, I hadn't had a squeak out of her.

"Penny and I were warm and cosy in the station waiting room. We could see what was going on in the coal yard by the light of a good moon. Megan the Signal had kindly unlocked the door after the last train had departed for Carmarthen. The back window overlooked the coal yard and we could see the loaded lorries waiting to go out first thing in the morning and the very scales upon which I knew every single bag had been weighed.

I had taken the first watch, while Penny, by the light of her little flashlight, was reading her latest loan from the library - the unbelievable exploits of James Bond – He's a master spy you know. I had to nudge her to ask, what is that contraption coming up the station path with small headlights on it?

She looked out of the window to see it coming into full view and said. "It's a pram complete with a couple of buckets on top. the lights are battery torches being carried by what I can only say are two contrasting and shadowy shapes. One large the other much smaller." We could only watch as they stopped alongside the nearest coal lorry. The larger of the two figures swung easily up onto the back and was examining the bags by torchlight. As they worked and turned their illuminating beams towards each other; their faces were now visible for the first time. Bron stifled a shriek and mouthed, 'Dai and Dafydd Thomas!'

The smaller of the two had unloaded the buckets and pushed the pram to one side."

As the murmurs in the church hall were circulating, it occurred to me that as much as we all had expected those two to be up to something, this was still a bit of a shock.

Penny took up the story. "We didn't make a sound as we watched them. Dafydd jumped down and took the nearest bag onto his shoulders, carried it over to the scales and lowered it carefully. He then returned to pick up a bucket, took a small shovel from the pram and walked over to an empty coal wagon. He started to fill the bucket with small pieces of leftover slack, mainly heavy dust from the bottom of the wagon. Dai was carefully removing lumps of coal from one side of the bag on the scales. He filled his bucket twice and emptied it both times into the pram. Dafydd returned with the bucket of slack. He emptied it down the inside of the bag on the scales until the weight came back up to the required level. Dai then pulled coal across the bag to cover the slack. Dafydd picked up the bag and put it back in its place on the lorry. Having collected their buckets and the shovel they departed, pushing the pram down the station path towards town.

Penny said, 'There goes Mrs Hughes's Nantgarw Bright. It's the quality of the coal that they're after.'

I agreed with her saying. "We now know why the coal level

dropped in the bag, the slack at the bottom is more tightly packed than the lumps at the top. One of Dai's bright ideas, don't you think?"

Penny gathered her belongings and said to me, 'Let's get after them to see where they are taking the spoils from tonight's misdeeds. For sure, they're not going through all this business and covering their tracks just to fill their grate at home."

The goings on in my husband's coal yard had given me a turn at the time and going through it all again didn't make it any easier.

I was pleased when Bessie intervened to suggest a 'tea etcetera' break as she liked to call them. It gave me time to recover and more importantly hand the proceedings over to Penny. In next to no time, all were back in their seats waiting for our Night Owl to unravel further our Nantgarw Bright mystery.

Penny spoke out. "I suggested that Glenys get herself home, she starts earlier than me. I followed our naughty boys down the past the park and along the Commons Road to a lock-up garage against the town wall. They took the pram inside and closed the door. I waited until they had lit a lamp and I could hear them moving about. I took care when I approached the garage and looked through the small side window. It was only then that I could see what they were really up to."

As I'd expected of a 'Night Owl' report being given to our circle, Penny paused to let the story so far build itself up. All present were listening intently and had moved from the sat position in their chairs to being perched.

Penny continued. "Dafydd was sorting out equal-sized lumps of coal and painting them with what looked like clear varnish. He then set them out to dry on a table not far from the window, shiniest side up mind you. Dai was folding a sheet of old newspaper, it looked like the Western Mail, and before my eyes, in less than a minute I'd say, he formed it into a small box. On the table was a stack of tissue paper which looked like the wrappers you get on oranges at Christmas. These had printed on them, Produce of South Africa, however, the word Africa had been inked out and replaced with Wales and there were lids, for the boxes I thought, made of folded sheets of the South Wales Echo."

Bessie the Law commented. "Seems to me that Dai's time in

Swansea Jail was spent in the library looking up Origami, the Japanese paper folding skill. This latest scheme was obviously hatched while he was paying the price for his last ill-fated crime."

She turned to Penny. "From what you've seen girl, any idea what they are really up to?"

Penny's face was flushed. "I know exactly what they are up to but I don't think I should tell you!"

Bessie was twiddling her thumbs. "This is getting to be a proper saga, before you eventually tell us what you think you can't, could you kindly explain why not?"

You could have heard a pin drop onto a carpet, Bessie had now moved the whole incident up a couple of notches.

Penny said. "If I tell you what happened next you would be an accessory after the fact. Well, half the fact really! I only committed half a crime."

Bessie lifted her hand. "You either did or did not commit a crime, why do you think it's only half."

"I'm not admitting anything to save you being implicated but I may have conducted a breaking and entering without the entering bit."

Maggie the Shop said. "This is worse than when Mrs Jones at Number Sixty Two, is dithering whether to surprise her husband with either streaky or fatty bacon for tea, just say it and if it's a problem we'll all have an attack of severe memory loss."

Penny explained. "I waited about an hour until the boys had departed, as I was getting up off my knees, I stumbled against the window causing the bottom latch to spring up. That was the breaking-in bit."

Bessie had returned to her patient self. "Did you actually climb in through the window?"

"I didn't but I switched on my flashlight and put my other arm in. I then closed the window allowing the latch to fall back into place."

"Why only your arm?"

Penny reached into her apron pocket and pulled out a piece of folded paper. "These flyers were on the table, but face down, so I took one to see what they were up to."

Bessie nodded. "Now we're getting somewhere, don't give that piece of paper to anyone else but you can read the important bits out loud to us."

Penny smoothed the paper out, she read,

"The South Wales Diamond Mining Company invite you to be part of history. Coal and diamonds are both formed from carbon over millions of years and this is your chance to buy a well-preserved piece of premium Welsh coal which has come from the very same seam as the one to be prospected. There might well be a diamond forming inside this keepsake as you own it. The estimates are that the Welsh diamond fields could well overtake South Africa as the leading producer of these rare gems.

If this family treasure is not as described, you will be entitled to a full refund. Please send a postal order for two shillings to PO Box 99 Pembroke Dock and your family heirloom will be delivered to your door."

Penny sat down.

I could see many heads were nodding around the sewing circle. Most I would think would agree with me that this had all the trademarks of a Dai Thomas shifty scheme designed to appeal to those who had reputations to build and money to waste.

Bessie looked satisfied. "That is a publicity flyer intended for distribution to selected households which are above themselves and no doubt within the public realm, so I don't think you'll get a summons for borrowing that to read. Your body didn't enter the garage and the window latch sprung off on its own accord. All in all, in my opinion as a serving police officer's wife you are still a law-abiding citizen. Now, what are we going to do to put a stop to this, without the wayward pair knowing that we are involved?"

Penny stood up again. "We've had a good think about that. Because of the need to break and enter, without doing either, we suggest that we only share our intent with one other person. With the help of Glenys the Coal and another little outing for both of us Night Owls, we are sure we can put Dai and Dafydd out of business."

I left the meeting a much happier woman indeed.

***

The members of the Station Road Sewing Circle, urged by the chair, Bessie the Law had 'Kept the Faith' for several meetings. I had reported that the coal bags were no longer being tampered with and that Mrs Hughes had no more complaints in her.

After a useful presentation by Florrie the Fire on 'Invisible stitching and knowing how to find out where you had left off', Bessie called our real meeting to order.

"Through connections best kept to myself, I have in my possession a flyer which was delivered last week to one of the homes selected by Dai and Dafydd. Ladies, I think we can safely say that the South Wales Diamond Mining Company is no longer and has ceased trading within the extended boundaries of Pembroke town."

She took a piece of folded paper from her skirt pocket,

"The South Wales Diamond Mining Company regret to inform you that we have had to withdraw our once in a lifetime offer, to celebrate our plans for the South Wales Diamond fields. The decision has been taken out of our hands by circumstances out of our control.

Our representative will call round later with your postal order, (None of which have been cashed to date) and put it through your letter box. As a gesture of goodwill, we ask you to keep the memento or better still, put it on your fire with our compliments."

There was no clapping, cheering or any such celebration, all present knew that there was still unexplained business. The Night Owls, Bron and Penny, at last, would be permitted to explain how they, with my assistance, put paid to the Thomas boys' latest get rich, or in their case get poor scheme.

Bron the Books gave the first insight. "Glenys kindly provided Penny and me with a quantity of slack and coal dust and a few averaged sized lumps of Nantgarew Bright. On my kitchen scales, we filled up a batch of small icing bags with slack to the same weight as the coal lumps. We sealed the bags and set off well after dark for Dai and Dafydd's garage. Having checked it was locked up, a sharp knock on the window released the catch. Penny gave me her flashlight to hold and being taller than me she reached in further and brought out as many of the completed boxes as she could, complete with a bit of

101

ribbon around each one."

She leaned back, looked at me and then Penny.

There's no denying it, I and the Night Owls were beaming with our handiwork.

Penny continued the tale. "When I pulled the boxes out, we undid them, removed the coal lumps and replaced them with a portion of slack and coal dust. We put the lids on and tied up the ribbons. I put them back as much as I could remember in the same place. We locked the window and left. We couldn't tell you what we had done until we were sure our scheme had worked. We're not sure if Dai and Dafydd had already received complaints or if they had spotted our coal dust creation before delivering many of the packages. Either way, their money-back guarantee ensured that at a minimum they will be out of pocket."

I reached under the table and pulled out a large brown paper bag. "I thought we might be able to celebrate with a cream cake or two, fresh from Halls the Bakers. I can promise you these were all made this morning, with not so much as a single speck of coal dust on any of them."

Out of the Frame – *Penny the Photo*

From the first time, I overheard someone refer to me as Penny the Photo I loved my new tally. It was the latest in a string of acceptances, which demonstrated that although I was a native of Cardiff otherwise known as from 'Up the Line', I had been welcomed into everyday Pembroke.

I had been able to join the Station Road Sewing Circle on two counts. When I decided to stay on in Pembroke after a long hot summer holiday, I initially worked in the fruiterer's shop on the East End Square and lived in a flat above it. The other reason that I gained entry to the exclusive sewing club was that I had learned to knit at a very early age under the strict teachings of my Irish grandmother who lived with us in Tiger Bay. My frequently sported, stitch-perfect, if I say so myself, knitted Aran jumpers attracted considerable attention at the Station Road end of town. Joan the Tip was my proposer saying 'That Penny the Photo, she's just what we need up here, you can tell the quality of her knitting a mile off.'

My tally came from my current occupation in Pugh the View's photography studio, more of a shop really with a big room behind it. My duties included assisting Mr Pugh to take family portraits and holding infants who had made it plain, one end or the other, that they were not ready to be captured on film. I accepted film rolls from the public and shared in their delight when returning the fully developed pictures, which it appeared had to be thumbed through before the happy subjects could leave the shop. More recently Mr Pugh entrusted me to attend weddings with him. I had not only demonstrated my willingness to carry some of the heavier cameras but I'd also developed the herding skills of a sheepdog in getting the right family groups in front of Mr Pugh's lens in the right order.

It was on such an occasion two weeks ago that my troubles began. I wasn't ready to involve the sewing circle at this time, even though I knew they would move mountains to keep the town and its reputation safe. The only people I could bring myself to share my woes with were my best friends Bron the Book and Florrie the Fire. We were the younger element as Bessie our leader referred to us and we enjoyed the weekly dance above Haggar's cinema. at which the other members of our sewing circle proudly stated they wouldn't be seen dressed up or dead.

Bron and I were always on the lookout for new talent, more hope than substance mind you, but Florrie was only there for the dancing. Her heart belonged to a confirmed bachelor, a member of the local fire brigade. Everyone in the town knew about her fruitless obsession with him but were all sympathetic enough never to mention it.

We were in the back of the library which had been closed from one o'clock as it was a Wednesday. Bron had produced a bottle of Blue Nun wine in response to me saying my circumstances were too far gone to be drinking tea. Florrie had taken the afternoon off from her job as the fire station clerk due to the seriousness of my plight and as soon as our glasses were full, I told them how the entire mess had come about,

"Mr Pugh was delighted to have gained the job of taking the wedding photos at Stackburton Hall on the road to Milton. We'd recently taken delivery of a long exposure travelling camera which he would use to capture the entire wedding party of one hundred and twenty guests. Mrs Deveraux-Collins, who adored being called Mrs DC, her late husband had made his money in electrical fittings, had announced that her daughter Poppy would have the best wedding ever seen in South Pembrokeshire. We had packed anything that wasn't nailed to the shop floor into Mr Pugh's Triumph Mayflower and arrived early. From the guest list provided by Mrs DC we knew the positions that everyone needed to be in for the big photograph."

Florrie stated. "I'm already at the bottom of my first glass girl, no sign of a crisis yet, I'll be well away by the time you get to the point of all this."

I smiled, Florrie was always in a hurry, usually behind a fire engine.

"Let me tell you about Dilys!"

She accepted a top-up from Bron and listened, her interest had returned by the appearance of a new name.

"As I was setting up on the front lawn a young woman about our age ran up to me and asked if I had a spare camera. She was nicely dressed but certainly not a guest. She explained that she worked for a portrait painter and that she was supposed to take a close-up photo of every single guest as they arrived. This was indeed a shock and a mystery to me not to mention Mr Pugh when he found out. I had thought the only record of the happy day would be from our cameras. According to Dilys, Mrs DC had engaged the society painter Auberry James from Tenby to produce one large oil painting depicting all of the guests. The portrait would then be displayed in the drawing room of her daughter's new home in Freshwater East.

Bron sniffed. "That's impossible – who ever heard of everyone in a wedding party standing still long enough for a portrait? He'd be better off waiting for your large group photo and using that to copy from."

I lowered my chin. "That's exactly what he plans to do but Dilys told me, for him to get more detail into each person, she must take their individual photo as they arrive. She was beside herself because she'd left their camera behind and Auberry had a bit of a temper on him."

Bron said. "Did you give her one of yours?"

"Of course, I did, we have several Kodak Brownies which weren't going to be used. I also gave her a box of films."

Florrie leaned back. "If I'm following you, this Dilys had an issue and you sorted her out. Why have I taken this afternoon off if the problem is already solved?"

I could see that I needed to get on with this,

"Dilys phoned the shop a week later and asked me to meet her in the Dak café in Manorbier. She was adamant that I had to be on my own."

Florrie beamed. "This is better, sounds like a 'Brief Encounter."

"You could say that but this was a secret meeting between two young women, not like the film."

Florrie had put her glass down. "Why the secrecy?"

"She gave me a photo of a young man that she had taken at the entrance to the wedding but she said he doesn't appear in our large photo. There are indeed one hundred and twenty guests in our picture and the portrait. She was worried sick about telling Aubrey that they have possibly left an important guest out. She asked me what should she do?"

Florrie chipped in,

"I hope you told her to rip up the photo, the guest was responsible for not being in the group photo, she should leave the matter there."

I concurred. "That's what I should have done, instead I told her to forget it and took the photo from her. I didn't rip it up though."

Florrie was by now enjoying the benefits of two full glasses of Blue Nun,

"I'm going to give up on you girl, that's the second time you've bailed her out. Why would you not do a simple thing like tear up a photograph."

I explained. "Because it isn't that simple",

I reached into the large camera box I had brought with me, took out a decorated casket and emptied the contents onto the table. The brilliance of the necklaces, rings, bracelets and brooches filled the room. "I found this in the bottom of the camera box when tidying up the day after I met up with Dilys."

Florrie's wine-fuelled flush had all but disappeared.

Bronwen spoke up. "You are right Penny girl, this is definitely not a simple matter. It's time we involved the total resources of the Station Road Sewing Circle."

***

I had briefed Bessie the Law before the meeting in St Michael's church hall. She stood up and announced. "Maria from Milan has kindly postponed her talk on the romantic influences that Casanova had on Venetian Lace-making so that we can consider without delay the circumstances of one of our members who is possibly facing a charge of grand larceny."

She turned to me, leaving no doubt in anyone's mind who the would-be master criminal might be.

I stood and explained the background and events leading up to a large cache of jewellery being in my possession. I outlined my dealings with Dilys the portrait painter's assistant and expressed my desire that she should be no longer involved in this matter. I would be seeking assistance on finding the mystery man and establishing if he had anything to do with the jewellery ending up in my camera box.

I turned back to Bessie. "Since I informed you of my situation, could you confirm that a casket had indeed been stolen from Stackburton Hall?"

Bessie shook her head. "I have conducted several accidental glances at Sergeant Evans's notebook, he being, not only my husband but our town's solitary policeman. I can confirm that no robbery has been reported of any such nature from the Hall since or before the wedding."

Joan the Tip pointed out. "We don't know if there's been a robbery or whether this extra guest has anything to do with it, have you brought the photo with you."

I pulled out several large photos. "I made a few enlarged copies in the hope that one of you may recognise him, we don't even know if he's local."

I passed them around. My heart sank each time a member took a good look and responded with a shake of their head. I needed to know what this guest had been doing when we were taking photographs on the front lawn.

Auntie Sian called out. "Could I have another look please?" Two or more copies were hurriedly thrust towards her. She held her chin. "He's older in this photo of course but if it's the same person, he was in the secondary school with my nephew, the blacksmith. If I remember rightly, they shared a fair bit of detention together, rebels they were."

I tried not to sound desperate. "Could we go by the Smithy on our way home to see if he remembers anything at all about him?"

***

I was explaining to Bron why we were striding with purpose down Priory Road in Milford Haven. According to Auntie Sian's nephew the man in the photo was known at school as Bad Boy Benjamin. He had been in trouble for most of his life right up to his family sending him off to finish his secondary education in a private boarding school. He survived up to the sixth form when it seems that he did something terrible and was expelled. His family took his disgrace badly and disowned him. He then took a job down at the docks in Milford Haven where he's lived ever since.

Bron was a bit out of breath. "Where did you learn all this?"

"Up to when he moved away from Pembroke, from Auntie Sian's nephew. As for the rest, Bessie knows the president of the Women's Institute here in Milford, so few well-placed enquiries amongst the ladies of the town revealed his address. We should find him at his lodgings; he doesn't work Saturdays."

Bron looked puzzled. "I still can't see how any of this is going to help you?"

I replied. "You will when we meet up with him?"

I stopped outside a house with a blue door. Bron lifted her shoulders and looked at me as if waiting for more information before she would take a single step up the path.

I sighed. "His full name is Benjamin Deveraux-Collins. He is the bride's estranged brother."

Bron touched my arm. "You couldn't make this up, could you?"

I turned and walked up the path to the front door and gave it two sharp knocks.

The man in the photo opened the door. I took in a deep breath,

"Good morning, Benjamin, my friend and I need to talk with you about what went on behind the scenes at your sister's wedding."

The colour drained from his face, he was well-spoken but fear was in his every word. "I only did what I was told to do. I needed the money."

I said "Could we come in? I don't think you'd like to discuss this on the doorstep."

He took us down a dimly lit passageway into what could be at best described as a tip of a room. He was clearly allergic to washing up or any kind of cleanliness come to that. I caught the look from Bron, and we both remained standing. He seemed to be anxious to explain that all that he had done was under duress. "My mother said that she would pay me to take the jewel casket and get rid of it. I was to dress as if I was a guest, to avoid attention. `One of your girls," he pointed at both of us, "unfortunately took a photo of me as I went around the back but I thought it would prove nothing. While the main photos were being taken, I was to remove the casket from my mother's dressing room and take it with me. I was supposed to throw it overboard when coming back over the ferry from Hobbs Point to Neyland."

Bron interrupted. "Why did the casket end up in my friend's camera box?"

"I panicked when one of the catering staff saw me coming down the back stairs with the casket under my arm, your equipment was there in the stairwell so I hid the casket under some film boxes and left in a hurry."

I cleared my throat. "One small problem here, why would your mother ask you to throw away such a valuable casket?"

He laughed bitterly. "She wants everyone to think she's been robbed. All of the jewellery is fake, paste, and imitation. She is going to wait a few more weeks while the excitement of the wedding dies down before she claims they've been stolen and collects the insurance money.

Bron asked. "Where are the original gems?"

"Sold a long time ago to pay off my late father's gambling debts. My mother believes in keeping up appearances, she is practically broke and couldn't really afford the wedding."

I wanted to know if this was a family affair. "Does your sister know anything about this insurance swindle?"

"Good grief no! Although she has a trust fund set up by our father, he didn't lose all of his money. She can access the fund when she marries, she didn't want a big wedding in the first place. It was all my mother's doing. She would do anything to impress her cronies amongst the county's finest."

His unspoken words conveyed to me how distanced he had become from his family.

Bron said. "We're done here, anything else that needs doing will be done back across the river."

Benjamin looked worried. "Will I be getting a visit from the police then?"

I assured him. "This is the end of the matter, you've merely been paid to move a casket from one room in Stackburton Hall to the ground floor stairwell. Your mother will assume it is sitting at the bottom of the Cleddau. She's biding her time before putting in her claim. I presume you won't be visiting the Hall soon?"

He shook his head. "She made it plain that this was a single transaction and that I was still the family's black sheep."

We let ourselves out, not before telling him that our visit had to be kept a secret. If it ever became known to anyone else, we knew where to send the Milford police."

**

Florrie looked every inch the part. Her buttons had been burnished, leatherwork polished and the soft doeskin material of her uniform couldn't be faulted for a single piece of fluff. With her unruly ginger hair tucked into her cap and carrying her clipboard in front of her, she would be instantly recognised as a member of the Pembroke Dock Fire Brigade.

I complimented her on her ideal appearance. "Mrs DC won't know what's hit her when you wallop her front door. The minute she sees you in your official uniform, she will be on the back foot for sure."

Florrie beamed. "Let's do this and I'll have his uniform back in its locker before he misses it. He's teaching at a fireman's training session in Carmarthen until tea time.

I wanted her to concentrate on keeping Mrs DC occupied while I restored things back to where they were. Florrie was beside herself having discovered when trying on the uniform of her heart's desire that they shared the same vital statistics accepting that her finished shape was far more graceful.

I told her. "I'll need ten minutes tops to go up the back stairs to put the casket where it belongs. I have a good idea where the room is, I went into the stairwell several times during the wedding day, her dressing room must be off the same staircase. Are you happy with what you're going to say?"

She glanced at her clipboard. "Standard fire inspection

questionnaire relating to a large gathering reported here several weeks ago. It can only be conducted in the presence of the property owner."

We were approaching the last bend in the driveway before the Hall came into view, I put my hand on her arm. "I know that impersonating an official could get you into deep water with the Fire Brigade but I'm hopeful that we can sort out Mrs Deveraux-Collins once and for all. I went through the gardens to the back of the hall. The tradesman's entrance was open as Benjamin had described; I took my time to make sure there were no servants about. According to Joan the Tip, who had cleaned there for a while they all met at this time for a late breakfast. I entered the room and placed the casket in the centre of the dressing table. I placed a card inside the lid and left. Florrie's attempt to deflect Mrs DC from the back of Stackburton Hall had worked a treat. Within twenty minutes, we were on our way back down the drive.

Florrie couldn't contain herself. "I thoroughly enjoyed being a brigade officer. I went through all the questions and even persuaded her to show me where the reception was held."

I asked. "Did you have any creaky moments at all?"

"I was well into my stride when I said she needed to put up some fire exit notices so that if there was a fire, and we all hope there wouldn't be, then she'd have no trouble claiming on the insurance. I then remembered what her whole scheme had been trying to do."

"Did she respond to your mention of insurance?"

"It was only a fleeting look, but she looked as if she had been caught out."

"For all her being full of herself then," I summarised, "she looked like a woman who had been driven into all of this by her own pride?"

Florrie concurred. "All self-inflicted I'd say, we've cleared you from any involvement but she's still having a wedding bill to pay."

I couldn't help smiling inside. "We'll see!"

***

I thought it best that Bron the Books should be the bearer of good news. She waited along with Bessie and myself until Maria from Milan had finally delivered her talk of how Venetian needle lace patterns had migrated into gentleman's collar ruffs due to the antics of Casanova in 1750.

The tea and cakes had been well sampled when Bessie stood up to announce,

"Further to the business of Mrs Deveraux-Collins and the unofficial guest at the wedding at Stackburton Hall recently, Bron here is delighted to be bringing you a most unexpected outcome from the restoration of the casket full of fake jewellery."

In a sentence, I thought Bessie has confirmed her reputation for saying straight out how things are, as opposed to what they appear to be.

Bron responded. "A regular visitor to my library is Avril, one of the maids at the Hall. I gained her friendship when I acquired for her a rare copy of Great Victorian Poisoners - Volume Twelve that is, which she assured me was out of spontaneous curiosity, more so than attending to her wandering-eyed boyfriend from Llanreath. Avril told me that there had been several late-night goings on in the drawing room above the servant's hall. She added that it was the custom that when Mrs DC called a family meeting in the drawing room, the servants took it upon themselves to assemble underneath. This was not of course eavesdropping as such, as they couldn't help hearing the loudest of exchanges. On the first occasion, it was attended by only Mrs DC and her daughter who had recently moved out to join her husband in a new detached bungalow overlooking Freshwater East. The meeting which commenced quite civilly, ended with the daughter marching noisily down the stairs and slamming the front door as she left. Their second meeting seemed to be well-mannered so no news was gained."

I wasn't surprised in the least when Bron stopped and looked around the room. Whether reading out stories in the children's section of her library or delivering new characters into a sewing circle report she wanted to be sure that everyone had kept up.

When Bron was satisfied, she continued. "The following morning Mrs DC called the servants together and said that they would have to re-open the daughter's rooms to welcome back the married couple. That was the least of it. The builders would be arriving during the week to install a larger bathroom, an additional dressing room not to mention a nursery for future events! Avril said the most unnerving thing about it all was that Mrs DC was behaving oddly. She was floating around the place, all smiles you see as if she didn't have a care in the world.

It didn't end there! The following night there was another meeting between mother and daughter but this time they were joined by Beryl's husband who is their family solicitor. The meeting above the servant's hall was conducted with polite and well-bred voices. Regretfully no further news had been gathered.

Bron looked at Beryl the Will. "I'm sure your husband doesn't do many late-night consultations, was there anything you can add for us?"

Beryl replied. "He was indeed out the other night, I asked him if anything was amiss. He said that it was all resolved now by the partial encashment of a trust fund. All to do with a family who realised they wanted to live under one roof.

Megan the Signals wanted to know more. "Sounds like the daughter read her mother's horoscope for her, but how did she find out about the jewel caper? Did Mrs DC confess?"

Bron smiled at me. "I think we can give the last word on this one to Penny the Photo."

I felt my face go red. "As you all know I like a good read into the night. Better than that I love a good quote. With apologies to William Shakespeare, I wrote my version of one of his quotes on a card which I placed inside the casket. I knew the first thing she would do on seeing the returned jewel box, once she had overcome the shock, was to look inside to see if anything was missing.

This is what I wrote on the card; *If the legacy you leave behind is built on a lie it will not be carried on, it will be buried with you.*

Bessie closed our meeting. "Thank you to all members who were able to assist Mrs Deveraux-Collins to come to her senses. We can only hope that if she ever decides to re-marry, she will settle for a marriage photo or indeed a portrait but definitely not the both of them."

Music from Above – *Carol from Chapel*

We had just received a handful of hints from Joan the Tip on how to read a complicated knitting pattern correctly. Her instructions also comprised of maintaining the pace of completing three rows, unwrapping a toffee, marking off your Bingo card and keeping up with the Caller. In some places up the line, it would be referred to as multi-tasking but in the Station Road Sewing Circle, it was simply getting on with things as usual. Normally, I find these little snippets useful and jot notes down in the little notebook which I carry in my handbag to remind me for later on. Two reasons were present which caused my handbag to remain closed on this occasion. Firstly, on a matter of principle, it wouldn't be appropriate for the Baptist Minister's wife to be engaged in a gambling topic and more to the point I was still dwelling on the catastrophe that had beset the Chapel on the previous Sunday.

I had to unburden myself and you might say that it was Florrie the Fire's bad luck to come and sit down next to me. She approached me carrying a huge slice of lava bread topped with farm butter and homemade jam. We settled ourselves comfortably in one corner of the church hall to enjoy our refreshments. I worried that I had made Florrie my captive listener but as it turned out she was the most suitable member with whom I could have shared my troubles.

"It was during the evening service that things got out of hand." I told Florrie. "My dear husband had delivered a thought-provoking sermon which seemed to have been well received by all the congregation. Then it was the turn of our organist Mr Trevor Neville, you know Trev the Nev. Well, he has always prided himself on leading the congregation into the next hymn with as few preliminary chords as possible. We had just rendered the second of the three verses in 'Bread of Heaven' when out of nowhere Trev played his three-chord introduction to 'Hark the Herald Angels sing'.

Florrie gasped. "And here we are in October!"

I pressed on. "Now here's the thing, Trev is also our choirmaster; his body of fine voices is trained to respond without so much as a single additional breath as soon as the appropriate chords are heard. The choir moved with ease into the carol, unfortunately, the change was not applied by the staunch Baptists in our congregation. If there were three verses to 'Bread of Heaven' then three would be delivered!"

I paused to allow Florrie a sip of her tea - I wasn't finished with this story by a long chalk. "The choir, in their efforts to please Trev the Nev raised the volume of their festive offering in an effort to lead the congregation. This was countered by the Baptist brigade singing even louder still. Florrie my love, it was a travesty of sound."

She smiled broadly. "Now, Carol the Chapel, what would the Almighty make of all that then?"

I shook my head and raised my eyes skywards. "We can only hope that He forgave us. After all, at least everyone was singing their hearts out. I don't know about taking the roof off, I think we nearly blew it sky-high!"

We chuckled together, with a warmth shown by long-standing friends formed over many years in our small community. I went on. "The truth be told, I was more worried about my dear husband, our Minister. You know you'll never meet such a devoted man but any kind of trouble in the chapel plays on his delicate disposition. He and Trev had a proper dust-up after the service. My husband said that Trev had not only brought the prize-winning choir into disrepute but had upset many amongst the devout. Trev maintained that he had struck the right keys saying that his 'nearest and dearest' had never let him down."

Florrie looked confused. "Which nearest and dearest is he talking about Carol?"

"The organ!" I replied. "Trev and the organ are the same age you see. He was born in the week that the organ was installed in the Chapel. They are both seventy years old."

I could tell by Florrie's elated face that she wanted to hear more as she said. "Him being an only child, the organ's the only nearest and dearest he has left on this earth!"

I concurred. "You're on the button there girl. This is practically a family matter for Trev."

"Did they agree on anything at all?"

"Trev said that my husband could bring down the organ tuner from Ammanford but that he wouldn't find a thing wrong with his beloved instrument."

Florrie swallowed the last morsel of her lava bread and observed. "Something has plainly gone wrong, but both men are too proud to look for the answer. It sounds to me as if it would be best to resolve things without your chapel business being spread about the town or indeed Ammanford, for that manner. Could we take a look tomorrow evening after I finish work?"

I wasn't entirely sure what she had in mind but the interest she was showing in my dilemma certainly made me feel better. Florrie is a good friend when all's said and done. I replied. "Your offer is well placed Florrie, but I wouldn't know one end of an organ stop from another. I can only play the basics in Sunday school on the piano."

Florrie was up and running. "No bother girl, I'll have a word with Auntie Sian before she leaves. She's retired now and she might even be rusty but she used to play the pump organ up at the Apostolic Church at the top end of Station Road. I'm sure she could put Trev's 'nearest and dearest' through her paces."

***

We were barely at the door of the chapel when Auntie Sian's eyes lit up. She walked quickly up the steps to the organ throwing her coat over the balustrade and sliding with ease onto the polished bench. Her feet moved smoothly over the pedals to set up a low volume. She had assured me that by adjusting something called a swell shutter we wouldn't attract any attention from passers-by who might think that there was a midweek service being conducted.

It was still a marvel to me that the glorious sound coming out of the vast instrument was all driven by an electric blower. Long gone were the days when Trev the Nev would punish any misbehaviour in

116

the choir by assigning the culprit to man the mechanical pump handle. Florrie and I sat in the front pews and listened to Sian's impromptu recital, mainly hymns with a bit of Bach thrown in. She stopped abruptly and turned to us,

"Bearing in mind I'm feeling like a donkey rider on the back of a thoroughbred, there's something going on in the lower registers."

Florrie snorted. "Don't be technical Auntie Sian, give it to us in plain Pembroke speak if you please!"

Sian dipped her chin. "Sorry girls, I've got myself carried away. This is the best I've played in years. There are two or three titchy pipes down the far end that are playing up."

She slid off the bench and walked towards the back of the organ. "Some of these small pipes have glass inspection covers so that the reeds can be kept tidy. I'll see if they'll come off."

Florrie and I had all but given up on the technical side of Auntie Sian's descriptions. My hope was that we could do something that would ease the tension between Trev and my husband. A scream brought us both to our feet and we dashed around to see Auntie Sian with a big smile on her face. Her pinafore was dripping wet all over the chapel floor.

"All three had water in them which poured over me as I removed the inspection covers." She pointed at the little pipes. "It's got to be deliberate!" We followed her gaze upwards to the roof

"No sign of daylight and the beams are dry, can't be a leak so it's sabotage alright!"

Florrie announced. "The first part of this mystery might be solved but who might have it in for Trev the Nev?"

I felt I had to defend Trev and our congregation. "He might be a pain from time to time but I can't think of a single person who would do such a thing as to fill those pipes with water."

Auntie Sian was gracious as ever. "The main thing is that we've discovered what's going on down here. unlike some who would have been happy to blame divine intervention. Truth be told though; we still have a mystery to solve."

Florrie spoke up. "Carol love, I think you should keep the chapel locked until next Sunday. Your service should run nicely and your husband's indigestion will have been settled. In the meantime, we

117

need to let the Sewing Circle know what's been going on."

***

Seeing as it was Auntie Sian that had found the watery cause of Trev the Nev's unwanted chords, I let her explain to the assembled sewing circle the events leading up to early on last Sunday morning. I then described to the now intently listening women the emergency which had proceeded the latest morning service,

"Florrie, me and Auntie Sian opened up the chapel to confirm that all was well. Remember now, the chapel had been locked all week. Auntie Sian had barely muted the organ and moved into the first verse of 'How great though art' when she shook her head and disappeared round the back of the organ No scream this time mind you, but a hushed announcement of 'I don't believe it!' Florrie and I rushed around to discover a large puddle at her feet, she had her Sunday best on and thankfully when opening the pipe covers, she had managed to dodge this latest deluge.

Auntie Sian took over the report to the sewing circle. "There had been six small pipes brimming with water. We emptied them so that the organ was ready for the morning service. We knew, that no one had been in the chapel and I was by now beginning to think that something up there is behind these watery goings-on. It was only when Florrie reminded us that there had been a thunderstorm last Wednesday night that we were persuaded it had to be rainwater. The beams above us were still dry but somehow the rain had penetrated the roof."

Beryl the Will, her husband is the town solicitor, made a logical suggestion I thought when she said. "We will have to arrange to be there the next time it rains heavily."

Megan the Signals couldn't resist. "Are you suggesting that we do a rain dance on the pavement outside?"

Beryl smiled. "That's a thought but more likely, we'll have to hope that the weather forecast is bad before next Sunday."

Florrie lifted her hand, most of us had been in school together and still followed this proven method of gaining everyone's attention. "I had a look in the Western Mail before coming to our meeting, sorry to say it'll be dry all week. That said, I think I could arrange for a downpour around eight o'clock on Thursday morning. Now ladies, you may well wish to see the spectacle for yourselves but bearing in mind that the efforts of the Station Road Sewing Circle are best kept under wraps, I would ask you for no getting there early to having the best viewing point. The last thing we want is an organised turnout. If of course, you happen to be on your way for an early morning shop on Thursday morning, then it's natural that you would stop for a minute or two to view the unusual. Carol, Auntie Sian and me will be inside the chapel waiting for the evidence to descend upon us."

I smiled to myself, with the three of us already inside, there would be without a doubt at least ten other women going about their business at exactly one minute past eight on Thursday morning on the pavement opposite the chapel.

***

Florrie was dependable, you could be sure of that! It came as no surprise to me when exactly at eight o'clock on Thursday morning I could hear the bell on the fire engine as it cleared the way right through the Green estate, across the Mill Bridge and up into the Main Street. Florrie had told us, that before the bright red vehicle had screeched to a stop outside the chapel the firemen operating the turntable ladder would have already extended it towards the rooftops. It would be minutes later that their hoses would be delivering a steady torrent of water onto the chapel roof.

Being the clerk to the Fire Station, Florrie had been given the responsibility of putting together the practice schedules. To ensure that every practice run would be treated with the same enthusiasm as a real emergency call, she was charged with keeping the destination of each practice call-out safely locked in her desk.

Auntie Sian called out. "Enemy sighted at twelve o'clock," I don't think she had ever forgotten her time spent as a lookout on the top of Pennar Hill during the war. She was pointing up at the main roof beam and then at the water dripping down and already filling the smaller pipes of the organ. No sooner than we had established where the leak was, the sound of water on the roof ceased. The fading voices of the firemen and the rumble of the turntable being retracted told me that Florrie's plan had been successful, both outside and inside the chapel.

I turned to her. "Well done girl, we now know that it's only the heavy weather which is getting through the roof. How's your head for heights?"

Florrie grinned. "If you mean getting out onto the chapel roof, no bother. Many an open day at the fire station you'd find me being carried down the turntable ladder as a willing trapped victim in a pretend house fire."

We went out through the back door and climbed up the fire-escape ladder on the side of the chapel tower. We reached the gulley between the two pitched roofs of the chapel and carefully stood on the brickwork plinths. Florrie went ahead intently listening to the instructions from Auntie Sian below us directing us to where the water had come through the roof. We couldn't see a thing wrong until Florrie tripped on the lead flashing. She leaned down to look closer for the leak and a section, the size of a ridge tile moved, then came away in her hand.

"Well now" she gasped. "You won't find many lead strips this short or as light."

She passed the piece of metal to me. "It's a sheet of tin bent over to fit the roof ridge and painted to look like lead." I turned it over. "Now there's a further mystery, it's embossed with the words 'Shell Oil'.

Florrie shook her head. "No prizes for guessing what this was in a former life, it's an oil can, cut down and turned inside out.

I found three more of the replica lead sheets. "Someone has gone to a lot of trouble to cover up the theft of lead off the roof. Wouldn't be surprised if this is unfinished business. Let's put them back in place for now and go down to talk this through with Auntie Sian."

We all sat down in the chapel. "To put it simply," I summed it up for us all, "we must find out where the lead flashing is going and even more so, where's the tin coming from!"

Auntie Sian added. "In the meantime, you and I can pop in every morning after we've had rain, to clear the pipes and keep the peace."

Florrie stood up. "I think we are done here in chapel, the

likelihood of your husband, the Minister having another dust-up with Trev the Nev has been reduced to next to nothing."

I assented. "I'm grateful to you both but that's only the half of it. I'm clean out of ideas on how to take this further. We need to report every bit of this back to the Sewing Circle. The more we involve the others the sooner we can pick up the trail of this rooftop robbery."

***

I was happy to let Florrie explain to the sewing circle how we had discovered the cause of the goings-on in the chapel. To be fair it was her act of getting the practice fire drill at the chapel arranged, not to mention her tripping on the tin sheets resting on the ridge of the roof that had solved the issue of water getting into the organ pipes.

I then asked the ladies in the sewing circle for ideas about how we could track down the villains who had stolen the lead off the roof and where's the tin coming from.

Myvvi the Dead was first to respond. "Seems to me that if they were getting hold of the oil cans locally with their shell imprint and all, then they'd be going over to Griff's garage on the Lower Lamphey Road, him being the only Shell garage in our town."

Everyone nodded in agreement. She added. "I need to have a service done on our hearse, it seems to be using a lot more petrol lately. Relatives are not keen on paying more to take their departed ones to their final resting place, it leaves less in the will you see. I could ask a few innocent questions of Griff and find out if he's the supplier of the oil cans."

"That's a good idea" I replied. I was sure that Myvvi would use all of her gentler skills to discover without raising any alarm if Griff the Garage was indeed an unsuspecting accomplice. It was a constant challenge in all of our mystery-solving to keep our involvement a secret.

Joan the Tip had no such worries. "I'd put half a week's family allowance on the lifted lead being sold to Sharkey Ward, the scrap dealer out at Hundleton. He'd be doing time in Swansea Jail for sure if his wife Donna hadn't been keeping him on the straight and narrow. My husband nips in to see Sharkey from time to time, they sometimes find a nice bit of scrap in the back of the dustbin lorry. Coming back to Donna, she's always asking me for a tea-leaf reading. I'll pay her a visit during the week and see if my bet on her husband being mixed up in this turns out to be a racing certainty."

I was delighted with Myvvi's and Joan's ideas and we all agreed to discuss the outcome at the next sewing circle meeting.

***

I hurried along Station Road to the church hall. I couldn't wait to hear what our two girls had been up to before I delivered my own amazing news. Mivvi and Joan stood at the front whilst the remaining eleven of us sat in a circle, sipped our tea and munched through Bron the Book's delicious black treacle tart.

Myvvi looked nervous and hesitated before she spoke. "Sorry to say, I didn't learn all that much from Griff the Garage." I felt my heart sink but listened on. "After I'd booked the hearse in for a service, I asked him if he had a spare oil can in which we could keep a drop of petrol, just in case we ran out in the middle of a funeral. He sent me around to the back saying that there was a pile of them amongst old car parts and engines. I rooted about but couldn't find a single oil can anywhere. Griff came out to see how I was getting on. He said that he'd had a similar request from a couple of workmen a few weeks ago but instead of taking one, they must have cleared him out. That, ladies, confirms that's where the tin came from and Griff didn't have a clue what they were going to be used for!"

She sat down looking a little dispirited, however, I tried to support her. "Well done Myvvi, that's a good result. We may not know who the thieves are but it's likely that's where they were getting the tin locally. Perhaps Joan here might well shed some light on where they were taking their plunder?"

Joan on the other hand was beaming. "I had a lovely time with Sharkey's wife Donna. She seemed pleased I had visited and was full of what was happening with the family. I think most visitors are workmen and she doesn't get the chance of a good chat often. She was pleased to report that business was on the up and was keen to show me around the scrapyard. It was a lot tidier than I'd remembered. Best of all she walked me past a locked cage in which I saw plainly several large strips of lead flashing."

All of us ladies leaned forward eager to hear more.

Joan was encouraged and went on. "I waited until I had read the tea leaves in her cup. I said that I could see continued good fortune coming her way from the shape that looked like a money bag. However, I pointed out the outline of a church steeple in her cup which called for me to share with her a cautionary tale. It was then that I introduced her to the Tale of the Haunted Pews."

I'll be the first to say that Joan has a lovely voice for storytelling but she did speak slowly, drawing it all out. It made listening carefully hard going but she didn't let us down.

"There was a small Lutheran church on the north side of the Preseli mountains, a family church it was, built by a German farmer who settled there in the middle of the last century. Long before the wars you see. He had a large family and they worked alongside their neighbours without any bother. Over the years the family became smaller, some went back to Germany and others married and moved away. The last remaining member passed away some years ago."

I'll be straight, I'm a true follower of history but Joan was definitely going the long way around to tell us about an empty church up on a mountainside in the north of the county.

She pressed on. "The new owners of the farm announced that the church would be deconsecrated and demolished as they didn't have a call for it. All the fixtures and fittings would have to be sold afterwards. Several days before the sale, a farm boy from Letterston broke in and helped himself to four pews. Not plain you see, but beautifully engraved as was the Lutheran fashion. I don't need to remind you that the pews had not been deconsecrated. They were sold on to a dealer in Fishguard and that was the end of it ... only it wasn't."

She paused and scanned each one of us to see if we were still listening. "That said, the farm boy hurt his back moving hay bales and was laid off for six months. The dealer ended up not getting paid for the stolen pews and then went bankrupt. Their shady dealings over the church pews had come back to haunt them."

Joan sat back allowing everyone to digest this tragic end. I could see my fellow sewing circle members letting their imaginations run riot about the wrath of God. As it was, being a minister's wife, I knew exactly where she was going with this.

Joan coughed gently to signal the approaching pinnacle of her report. "Last Friday I was in the queue at Smith's the butcher's when Donna came in behind me. Mrs Evans at Number Seventy Two was up the front dithering over sausages again so we had time for a little chat. Donna said that she hadn't fully believed in tea leaves until she had asked Sharkey where the latest strips of lead flashing in their yard had come from. He said that he had bought them fairly from two roofers who were repairing leaking chapels between their normal slate work. That was enough for Donna, she told Sharkey to return the lead and to have nothing more to do with them. That's all that went on in the butcher's really, although I did go halves with her on the remaining six pork and leek sausages left by Mrs Evans."

I smiled as Joan teased us before her final delivery. "It would be fair to say that because Sharkey refused our thieves a reason for returning the lead and insisted that it goes back where it came from, or he would have a chat with Sergeant Evans, the thieves knew their game was up.

I chipped in. "I went up on the chapel roof this morning to make sure that the tin strips hadn't moved. Much to my surprise the lead had been replaced. Fair to say, the Chapel roof is now intact and it's in a better condition than when all of this business started.

The sewing circle erupted in loud applause which, when it finally subsided allowed Joan to conclude. "I'd bet the other half of my family allowance, on those two never repairing a roof in Pembroke ever again."

Going up in Smoke – *Florrie the Fire*

Tired didn't even start to describe how I was feeling. I was exhausted and leaned back in my chair trying not to close my eyes at the very moment that Beryl the Will was rounding off her excellent presentation. She had shared with us the challenges her old Singer sewing machine had given her whilst completing the beautifully stitched baby's quilt which she had laid out on the table for all of us to see. Me, being a single girl and all doesn't mean that I don't find babies interesting, my overwhelming fatigue was more to do with the boys who had been called out eleven times in the last week.

Glenys the Coal came to my rescue carrying two cups of tea. She sat down beside me saying. "You look rough Florrie love, I've put two extra sugars in yours to stop you falling off that chair." She put the cups on the table. "Now then girl, what's happened to the red-headed life and soul of our party?"

"Well now Glenys", I began. "I would be the first to say that my job description as the fire station clerk does not call for me to follow the fire engine every time there is a local shout. I can't help it if I feel compelled to see the boys in action and then again to observe their safe return to the fire station, can I?" I watched Glenys nod in agreement.

I lowered my voice. "I'll admit that I do have a particular interest in the Fire Station Chief who apart from being a magnificent leader in all fire matters, is up to now a confirmed bachelor". Glenys gave me a wry smile and I continued, "that aside, it's not only me who is being affected by all this business. Mrs Meredith at Number Fourteen has already sent in a written complaint to the Fire Chief. She said that she is currently living in wartime conditions well after the hostilities have ceased. The purpose of her wrath-peppered note was to highlight the frequent absence of Bevan the Paintbrush, him being a part-time fireman. Due to his callouts and the rest days he takes off to recover, he has left her with a three-quarters stripped front room not to mention the gaping holes where chunks of plaster have come off with the old embossed paper.

As if that wasn't bad enough, on my way here to the Station Road Sewing Circle, I was accosted by Mrs Pendleton at Number Seventy-Three who complained that Barry the Flush, another of our voluntary firemen, had disconnected her top water tank and had yet to return with a something or other connecting piece. If he doesn't replace it before Friday, it will be two weeks exactly since she's been able to have a proper bath!"

We both laughed and sipped our tea. "We've had a string of callouts without a single day in which to recover. Fires are breaking out all over town."

Glenys showed her concern, she was good like that. "You poor thing, I heard about the fire in Pembroke Dock at the back of the Woollen factory, took a few hours to get that one under control. I put that down to their preference for using only Welsh wool, those bales were no doubt excellent burners. Second only, mind you, to the Nantgarw Bright coal which my husband delivers all over town!"

I responded. "It isn't as if it's only a couple of kids up to mischief, these fires are ranging from the rubbish in a bin, to having to send both of our fire engines. To add insult to injury they occur at opposite ends of town, sometimes within an hour of each other. There must be more than one lunatic running around with a match in his hand."

"Surely the Fire Chief has called in Sergeant Evans?" Glenys raised her pencilled in eyebrows. "Not much gets past him in Pembroke."

I had to agree. "They have had a meeting in the office but from what I heard through the open window the Sergeant said it was too early without proof or witnesses to prove that they were at all connected. Until he could get around to investigate them further, they would have to be put down to a series of unfortunate coincidences."

Glenys snorted. "I bet the Fire Chief wasn't having any of that then!"

My voice went low. "The Chief didn't want to start a row, they're friends you see, so he nodded his agreement. However, what he then wrote in the Fire logbook after the sergeant had left conveyed his true opinion."

Glenys was practically sitting on my lap as she urged me. "Go on then, what did your man have to say?"

I whispered. "He printed his comments alongside every single call-out, underlined they were - *Very suspicious indeed.*"

Glenys sat up straight. "More mysterious than suspicious if you ask me. I think you need to get yourself home and catch up on your sleep. I'll ask around the ladies if they know anything about the fires. I'm sure our grapevine will turn up a few interested parties. I'll meet up with you tomorrow evening in Brown's café, it's quiet on a Tuesday. See you at six."

I went the long way around to go home down across the Commons Road, I couldn't face another word of interrogation from Mrs Pendleton, freshly bathed or not. I was truly ready for my bed.

***

Having received the well-sung benefits of Ovaltine the night before, it knocks me out every time, I felt much better as I stirred my milky coffee waiting for Glenys the Coal.

Right on time she came through the door of Brown's café followed by Megan the Signals and Maria from Milan. It seems that the fires had singed the lives of at least a few of the Sewing Circle members. I waited until they had armed themselves with teas and a late-in-the-day treat of an iced doughnut each, before I set the scene with a simple. "Well then Girls?"

Glenys spoke first. "I was handing out the delivery notes to the coalmen this morning when I mentioned the fire at the Woollen factory and said it's a good job we only deliver coal and not wool that flares up easily. That said, one of the men said he found a couple of charred newspapers in a coal bunker on Mansel Street yesterday when he was about to fill it up. He left them under the coal. If Mrs Saunders hadn't used up every last piece of coal, whoever had set fire to the papers, could have started a proper bonfire and a half. Then he added the most interesting fact I thought. The newspapers were the previous Friday's copy of the Western Mail. He couldn't imagine that anyone

127

would want to read one right through, never mind the two of them. Made him think they had been bought for more than just reading." She sat back waiting for the others to make their reports.

Megan the Signals finished off her tea, put down her cup, and looked straight at me. I surmised that she was about to fill in some serious gaps. "My sister, the one who I visit every week, she still lives in Narberth you know, is married to an insurance agent. A dour man is Devlin Harris, known to be over-cautious with his company's money. She said that he is merely a misunderstood and conscientious man who has a reputation for going by the book and sometimes over the top with it. Whenever he receives a claim he earns his tally well, he is known to many as Devlin the Detail."

Megan paused; she likes her audience to keep up. "One of his clients is the Woollen factory in Pembroke Dock and he told my sister that they had called him ahead of their pending claim. On the face of it he was going to have to pay out for the lost wool. The Manager said he would provide absolute proof that the blaze was started deliberately. Mind you, Devlin true to form, said that he would need to be convinced that the fire-raiser wasn't one of the workers having a quiet smoke around the back. That doesn't constitute arson in his book."

Maria from Milan piped up. "Your sister's husband is not being fair in other cases too. He also looks after the insurance for Lordsacre Farm. It's Georgie Rossiter's place as you know, where my husband is the milkman. Your brother-in-law said that the haystack, which was burned to the ground was due to Georgie's own doing. He said that the hay had been stacked during a wet spell and due to specific confusion or something like that, the haystack had set fire to itself. Cases of self-firing he insisted were not covered in the policy."

I was sure that she meant spontaneous combustion. "That can happen," I concurred. "never heard of it around Pembroke though. What did the Fire Brigade say was the most likely cause?"

"They arrived after the fire had gone out, nothing to see but ashes."

She looked at me then down at her feet. "Both fire engines were busy elsewhere and because there was no threat to life or limb, they came over after they had damped down the other blazes."

128

I had to stick up for the firemen. "Thankfully it only resulted in Georgie losing his cattle feed, we should be happy that no one has been injured."

Maria put her hand on my forearm. "If it was only that simple, Georgie has decided to cut back so that he can buy in more hay." Her voice was breaking. "He will be taking over the milk round three days a week and has told my husband there's a vacancy for a part-time stockman over in Penally."

Glenys gave Maria her hankie. "It can't be that upsetting love, your husband is a hard worker, He'll be taken on like a shot."

Maria looked forlorn. "Ever since we came to Pembroke from Italy my Antonio has set his heart on opening an ice cream parlour. What he doesn't know about making milk into ice cream you could fit on the sharp end of a carpet tack, whatever that is. When it comes to cows though, he only knows where the grass goes in and the milk comes out. We'll just have to tighten our belts."

I wanted to build on the little we knew. "Maria, you live in Kingsbridge Cottages, close to the farm. Could you have a good look around the burnt-out haystack to see if there is any clue on how it may have been started? Megan, could you possibly pay your sister an additional visit and bring up the business of the payout to the Woollen factory? It would be good to know what the proof was that the factory manager sent over to her husband. Glenys love, there won't be much to see in the filled-up coal bunker of your customer, but you could pay her a courtesy visit to see if the coal is up to scratch. You could then ask her if she knew how the two copies of the Western Mail could have ended up in her coal bunker. I'm going to do two things. For the moment I'll do my best to stop following the fire engines and work with you to find out who is responsible for these fires and I'll pay an early morning visit to Gwilym the News, to see how his sales of the Western Mail are going on."

***

There had only been four fires since our last meeting in Brown's café. A couple of cardboard boxes against a garage wall up Golden Hill, two dustbins over in Orange Gardens, one of which was a false alarm and a blazing bonfire at the back of Powells Removals. Old man Powell was more than put out when he discovered that the blaze had claimed over one hundred and fifty of his best tea chests, more commonly used as packing cases. There was a mass move coming up with the release of the new council houses on the Green estate and for the first time in many a moon, his large vans would be noticeably absent.

I was fully rested, having resisted the temptation of following the fire engines on their calls and I picked up the findings of the girls throughout the week. I was eager to share our better understanding of the mystery with the other members of the Station Road Sewing Circle. I arrived early to the Sewing Circle Meeting and requested Bessie the Law to announce that any other business would be conducted at the start of the meeting. I asked Maria from Milan if she could report first, it was best I thought to get all our findings out and then draw out any conclusions.

Maria stood up and said. "There was very little to see where the haystack had been, I poked around in the ash for some time but there was nothing that caught my eye. Then I remembered that my husband Antonio had said due to a stiff breeze on the night of the fire, the flames had taken hold quickly and that there would have been little left for the fire brigade to put out even if they had arrived earlier. I decided to search the hedge around the field and I found this." She pulled a small piece of baking parchment from her skirt pocket and carefully unfolded it to reveal a piece of singed newspaper. My heart sank as she held it up and said with no satisfaction. "Apart from the slight smell of petrol I can't make head nor tail of this, on one side is the bottom of a picture, I think it might be a team photo, the caption underneath says 'Well done the Scarlets'. On the other side, it's written in a foreign language."

Beryl the Will, leaned across and asked if she could have a closer look. She turned the piece of paper over. "It's Welsh," she announced, no surprise there she being the only fluent native speaker amongst us. "It's an obituary for a ninety-five-year-old, that was, from the village of Felinfoel. It's not far from Swansea where I used to live." Beryl handed back the piece of paper, Maria sat down.

I waited for the murmurings about a foreign influence to die down, then signalled for Glenys the Coal to share with us her result.

She announced. "Not a lot to say really. "I went round to Mrs Saunders at number seventeen for a friendly cup of tea. It was in her coal bunker you see, that the driver had said he found the charred newspapers in. We covered a lot of ground in our chat, from the cost of a dog licence to how much we both missed a nice tin of Spam now that the Americans had gone home. When I asked if the paper boy had been with her Western Mail she became a bit ruffled, saying that she had never had a local paper delivered to her house in her entire life and that in her opinion anyone who couldn't be bothered to walk down to Gwilym the News to get the Daily Herald was probably better off with the Dandy or the Beano."

All of us sat around the table smiled and a few rewarded Glenys with a gentle laugh.

I asked Megan to share how she had fared up the line. "On the day I visited my sister in Narbeth, my brother-in-law Devlin the Detail was down in Pembroke Dock presenting the Woollen factory manager with a cheque for his fire-consumed wool bales. My sister said it hadn't been the best of mornings, her husband had declared that giving away his insurance company's money was indeed a taxing experience. She didn't know where the tax came into it but the evidence presented to her husband had proven that the fire had been started deliberately by persons unknown."

She paused, Megan is Megan after all, she could make a sermon out of a shopping list, she continued. "My sister said it was several pages of newspaper, twisted into a kind of rope and it had a faint smell of petrol. Must have been dropped by the fire-raiser you see. It was however not a copy of the Western Mail!"

She looked around at all of us, probably to ensure that we were suitably hooked into her revelation. "It was indeed part of the Llanelli Star!" She sat down amongst the further murmurings going on over the astounding confirmation that at least one of the fire-raisers was from up the line.

All that remained was for me to make my report, I was confident that between us we had started to peel the layers off this particularly mysterious onion. "I popped into Gwilym's to pick up the early edition of the Western Mail and much to my surprise Doris his wife served me. She usually takes over from her husband after the morning rush. She saw my look and explained that he had messed up again, for the second time in as many weeks. He had sold a dozen copies of the Western Mail to the first customer in the door, which meant that several regulars had to go without. I was sympathetic to her situation of course, and said, 'Ah, these men, all they think about is how much is going in the till'. Mrs Gwilym leaned across her counter at me and said that she wouldn't have minded but when she found out who had bought the papers on both occasions, well, she thought her husband would have thought twice about it. It was none other than Dafydd Thomas, who most people in Pembroke know can hardly read one - never mind twelve newspapers."

I went on to explain to the girls that I had wanted to dig deeper but there was by now a queue of workmen behind me waiting to buy their papers and a packet of twenty.

"I decided that any part of the mystery relating to Dafydd Thomas could well be solved on home territory, so I thanked Mrs Gwilym for her time and hoped she wouldn't have to fend off customers ever again with surplus copies of The Daily Mail."

I sat down as the room split up into several conversations. I was happy to let this run and I could hear everyone coming up with their own conclusions. This gave me time to think through our next step. I cleared my throat and everyone fell silent. "It is now clear to me that we are dealing with the Thomas brothers, Dai and Dafydd".

I smiled as I reminded myself of the previous encounters we'd had with the naughty boys of Pembroke. There's a gap of one year between the two young men but the difference between them couldn't have been greater. Dai is bright and comes up with all their ill-fated money-making schemes and Dafydd is the strong-man. "We may not have found out much about the third party in this conspiracy," I concluded, "but in line with the Sewing Circle's intent to keep the people of Pembroke and Pembroke Dock for that matter, safe in their beds, we will first have to save the brothers from themselves". It was time I thought for a cup of tea.

⁎

I signalled to Bessie the Law to bring us all to order. She only had to raise her hand the once.

I announced. "Before I give you my thoughts on where we go from here, does anyone have anything to add?"

Carol from Chapel put her hand up, funny that, habits from when we were all in school together never seem to change. She said. "One of the dustbins you mentioned in Orange Gardens belonged to a member of our congregation; she is a light sleeper and was out of her back door before the flames had taken hold. She put the lid back on the dustbin and the fire went out. You won't be surprised to learn that one of the Western Mails from Gwilym's had ended up on top of her rubbish."

I responded. "That fits in with my thinking. Our boys have been setting alight what I would call diversions while the third party as we call them has been causing the most damage".

Bessie chipped in. "It's quite likely that the wayward brothers are following their aim in life of doing the least work to make the most money. We need to deal with them first. Bearing in mind that our activities in these matters are best kept a secret, I recommend that we bring on the Night Owls."

I nodded approval and then looked at Penny the Photo and Bron the Books who had both smiled their consent. Neither of the young women graced their beds before midnight. Penny a photographer's assistant, who sometimes still did modelling work held the belief that when she was asleep, she had very little control over her body. She preferred her waking hours more to ensure that she didn't neglect her slender shape.

Bron thought it natural for the town librarian to eat, sleep and read books right to their very end all in one sitting. I'd be surprised if she could count on both hands how many times she had stayed up all night to discover who had done what to whom, when and with what.

I followed my train of thought. "We know from experience that the brothers' preferred working day is between midnight and two in the morning. If the Night Owls can follow them and see if they are meeting with the other party in this piece, we'll have a better idea about how to stop them".

Carol's hand shot up again, I didn't mind, she looked excited. "If the boys are only lighting small fires, can we put them out before the firemen are called out? Dai, him being the brighter of the two would realise that someone is on to them. That should cause enough panic for them to warn off the other party."

Bron agreed. "Spot on Carol, I've just received a new fire-fighting appliance from the Local Authority. Would you believe it, the latest gadget is a big woollen blanket which has been soaked in chemicals to stop it from catching fire. I think it's because they couldn't bear the thought of all our lovely books going up in smoke."

Penny was ready to go home and change. She couldn't wait to start her late-night vigil. Understandable really, she's always had a thing about wearing black.

Carol suggested that we meet in the chapel later in the week for a catch-up. With so many of the Sewing Circle becoming involved in solving this emerging crime, she said we'd never all fit onto one table at Brown's café. I thought that was a good idea as we could gain too much attention if the next meeting was held there.

***

It's amazing what plenty of sleep can do for your well-being, I was up and ready to go the moment I sat down in one of the front pews in the chapel. All the members of the Sewing Circle involved in our efforts to flush out the fireraisers were present.

Penny gave us the Night Owls' report. "We have followed the Thomas brothers for three nights. The first they spent picking up spilt coal from the station yard and taking it home in a pram. Too much for their own use we thought, probably selling it on to their neighbours."

Glenys the Coal muttered. "I must get the coalmen to look where they're shovelling!"

Penny continued. "On the following night they went out and set fire to two bins and two piles of rubbish at the back of houses on the Green estate, all of which we were able to put out as soon as the brothers had moved on. Bron's fire blanket certainly did the business for us."

I smiled at her and said. "No wonder there has only been one call-out this week, that was to Griff's garage on the Lower Lamphey road. Funny thing though, only a small pile of used tyres was set fire to. A larger stack waiting to be sent up the line was untouched. Truth be told, when Griff switched on a light to have his favourite midnight snack, a prime Welsh bacon sandwich, his doctor told him to ease back on the fat you see, he may have disturbed them. Griff that is, not the Doctor"

Bron had leaned forward. "Would you like us to tell you the best bit."

I blushed, couldn't help it. "Sorry about that, I was joining up a few bits there."

Bron put her hand on my arm. "No worries Florrie, what we've found out will cap it all. On the third night, the brothers checked out the fires which they had started the night before, they must have known there were no call-outs. They looked confused not to mention concerned. We had collected the remnants of all the Western Mails they had used to start the fires. They went to the phone box at the bottom of the Green estate and asked the operator to put them through. After a fair bit of shouting Dai slammed down the phone and they set off home. Penny followed them and I nipped into the phone box to call Maisie the night operator, didn't give my name but told her I had been cut off, could she tell me the number so that I could call them back? She was very obliging. I think she wanted to get back to one of her nightly cat naps."

Penny added that before the Thomas brothers had reached their home, she had overheard Dai saying to his brother, 'We'll stick to our own schemes from now on!'

Bron stood up in front of us, she hadn't finished, and the chapel roof amplified the silence awaiting her final revelation. "It was a private Swansea number, which I called this morning. A man answered saying he was Garry Everett. He then said - Sales Representative for Star Mutual Insurance. That was good enough for me. I rang off."

Megan the Signals sat bolt upright. "Devlin, my brother-in-law, works for Provident Farmers Insurance, I'm sure. This other lot must be his competition. Would you believe it, all of this is intended to turn Devlin's customers against him?"

Maria from Milan's voice was wavering. "My Antonio is the victim of an insurance war, if his job wasn't threatened, I'd say this was exciting."

I was half excited you could say, we had saved the naughty boys from another possible spell in Swansea prison. It would have done their mother in. All we had to do is put Mr Everett in his place and this fiery episode in Pembroke's history would be extinguished so to speak.

I turned to Bron. "Could you find out from the address clerk at the exchange where our Mr Everett lives? I would think a little anonymous parcel containing the charred remains of the Western Mails collected by the Night Owls accompanied by a printed note will send him running. Joan's son still has his John Bull home printing kit. The note should say that neither Mr Everett's fire-raising activities nor his insurance policies will find a welcome the next time he shows his face in West Wales. What do you think girls?"

All present clapped and complimented each other on how we were going to bring the fireraisers up short without revealing a single initial of who we were.

I put my hand up. "There's a little bit of unfinished business. I would suggest that Maria leaves her scrap of the Llanelli newspaper down on Lordsacre farm where her husband or Georgie Rossiter the Midnight Farmer will find it. With all the fires that we've had across Pembroke, I'm sure they will be contacting Devlin the Detail to persuade him that they have a genuine claim. Your husband Antonio," I smiled at Maria, "can then look forward to a full week of delivering our milk."

The second round of unplanned applause was louder. We were called to order by Carol. "Now then girls, keep it down, if my husband the Minister hears you from the vestry next door, he'll be wondering what kind of prayer meeting is going on in here."

We filed out onto the Main Street, giggling we were, but all the same, looking as pious as we could.

136

A Pearl Set-Up – *Joan the Tip*

Being the mother of four growing boys calls for a string of never-ending obligations. Satisfying their increasing appetites, mending uniforms after the scrapes they get into on their way home from school and clearing up after them, in general, are certainly top of the list!

My only relief comes in two guises: firstly, being a leading member of the Station Road Sewing Circle, where my keen interest in knitting has helped others to polish up their casting skills and to slip a stitch or two smoothly. The other brief break in my busy life is when I'm collecting the family allowance from the Post Office every Tuesday. It's not the short exchange I have with Marion behind the counter, she rarely has any news in her. However, I'll admit that I am partial to a bit of information collecting. Popping into Browns Café next door to enjoy a quiet cup of tea and a chocolate éclair is a delight. Some might say that it's nothing more than gossip. I would say it's keeping up with what's going on in Pembroke on behalf of our sewing circle. It's these small snippets the thirteen of us bring to the meetings that help us to keep the town tidy and ensure the inhabitants can sleep safely in their beds.

That said, I was somewhat intrigued by a mysterious incident last week which involved me being nothing short of interrogated by a complete stranger. I only started to worry after chatting with two other members of our sewing circle when I learned they had also experienced a similar exchange. They persuaded me to bring the matter to the attention of Bessie the Law. Her tally comes from being the wife of the town's solitary policeman; she also happens to be our sewing circle leader.

Bessie listened intently to my report which outlined my chance meeting at the café and those of Beryl the Will and Megan the Signals. Much to my surprise Bessie recommended that as I was the first one to endure such an encounter, I should bring the subject up during our next meeting and share our revelations with those present.

***

I bided my time at the meeting until after Maggie the Shop had announced that she had written the latest pantomime script to be performed here in Saint Michael's church hall. Between us we had then decided who would make the costumes to fit the cast of seven adults and the traditional pint-sized extras drawn from the East End Infants School.

I stood to address the group and announced. "I was minding my own business, and a little bit of other people's, as I was sat in Brown's café on Tuesday last". I paused and observed the exchange of knowing glances between several of the ladies.

"A woman, in her forties put her cup of tea on my table and said 'May I join you?' There were plenty of empty tables but as the conversations that I'd listened in to hadn't produced a scrap of decent news, I welcomed her. I'm telling you now girls, she wasn't from around here. She was wearing a full set of pearls, a necklace and earrings to match. It was a dead giveaway if I've ever seen one. We all know that pearls should only be worn at weddings and funerals. She didn't have a buttonhole flower and she wasn't wearing black, so it was clear to me she was from out of town. She had a proper Welsh accent mind, so I was sure that she must be from up the line or at least from over the other side of Carmarthen."

I could see some of the girls shifting in their seats, I might have overdone the stranger's introduction.

"Now here's the thing, I've never seen her in all my life but she talked to me as if she knew more about me than she should. To be fair though, I only realised that later on what was really happening."

They were all now leaning forward in their seats, hanging on my every word as I revealed the mystery. I continued. "After several sips of her tea the stranger asked me, 'Could you give me directions on how to get to the Town Hall?'

I obliged her. "Left out the door, stay on this side of the pavement, straight down the main street for twenty yards, Campbell's garage is on your left side, twenty yards further you will pass Mendus the Chemist, beyond there you'll see Haggar's Cinema and finally go past the Castle Inn to find the Town hall on your left!" I added. "If you pass the Lion Hotel, you've gone too far!"

"She looked at me with a bit of a smile on her and said, 'Goodness me, there's a full set of directions, are you so detailed in everything you do?' I replied with all the modesty in me that it's no good knowing where you are and where you want to get to if you've no idea what's in between."

"She said it was a bit like a complicated knitting pattern, 'you can have the needles and the wool but you'll never make a jumper without understanding the instructions'. Well, now my back went up, so to speak. I began to think that she was after more than directions to the Town Hall. I told her, as it happens, I have over the years discovered a few tips to make sure that a knitted garment, however intricate, is tidy but I share the pointers mainly with my crafting friends." Everyone in the room smiled.

"She didn't seem to get the message that I wasn't in the habit of sharing my experience with strangers and she pressed on, 'Would you have any handy hints that you could share with me?' I have to say I was a bit short with her by then and said Two Sharp Pencils!"

"I thought that would be the end of it but she insisted, 'Don't you use knitting needles then?' She was giving me as good as she was getting! I spoke more seriously and explained that if it's a complicated garment, you should use one of the pencils to mark where you are on the pattern every time you stop. She asked what the other pencil was for and with such a straight face, I said in case you break the point of the first one"

"She laughed out loud, I'll give her that. Then after a few more questions about knitting, she said she'd taken up enough of my time. Just as she was leaving though, she said I'd be the ideal person to fill in any form accurately and that my attention to detail is more than commendable. It was only then that I realised what she was up to!"

If you'd dropped a knitting needle on a Welsh lambswool carpet you would have heard it, an explanation was being waited for.

"You all know that my husband drives the dustbin lorry here in Pembroke. The money's not big but he's happy enough to work with a good gang. To make sure that I and our four boys don't go without he turns his hand to a bit of woodwork. The jobs he does on the side are just enough to keep us from wanting. They don't amount to much, so we don't bother the taxman. It's occurred to me, in view of her form-filling comment that she could be from the tax office in Cardiff. One of their random inspections I wouldn't be surprised."

I had a little more to say on the matter. "It came to my attention during the week that I was not the only one in our sewing circle to have been accosted by Mrs Pearl-Set. I call upon Beryl the Will to tell you what happened to her."

***

Beryl stood up. "I've had a similar experience to Joan. I didn't get to share a cup of tea with our mystery woman, my encounter with Mrs Pearl-Set was on the steps of the Town Hall, would you believe it, on Thursday morning."

Her broad Swansea accent I thought, even after living in Pembroke for seventeen years, added a musical lilt to her report. She continued. "The Town Hall has never been busier. Everywhere you look in the borough they are putting up council houses. My solicitor husband, the Town Clerk, said to me that the paperwork you have to go through is enough to paper the walls of each and every dwelling being built! He has been going to work earlier and leaving later for months now. He is working against the clock and can't catch up. The poor boy is so worn out. He went into work on Thursday without his bulging briefcase. Stuffed full of plans and permissions it is, more like a suitcase really. I handed it into the receptionist, a nice girl from Monkton, who I have to say though, was wearing her lipstick a bit too vermilion for my liking. Coming back to my odd exchange, it took place when I was on my way out."

I saw Beryl take encouragement from the enwrapped expressions on all our faces. She knows only too well, that the inner workings of the town council are nothing short of covert and cryptic to all of us, so any insight she had gained on Thursday morning would be more than welcome. Unfortunately, we were to be disappointed on that aspect but her conversation with the strange visitor was far more fascinating.

"There she was at the bottom of the Town Hall steps." Beryl was back into her stride. "The lady in question was wearing a green two-piece and I must say her pearls set it off nicely. She was standing on the middle of the bottom step; I couldn't have gone around her if I'd tried. It was almost as if she had been waiting for me to come through the revolving door. 'Could you kindly describe to me how I can walk to the railway station?' she asked me. My first thought was - there's a Rhondda Valley's girl if I'm not mistaken.

Mrs Pearl-set added, 'These court shoes are made for looking at and not for long-distance walking. I would appreciate your most direct instructions.' Well, I politely said it's straight up through the middle of town from here and take the first right after the railway bridge. I was happy to leave the conversation at that but as she stepped back on the pavement to let me go through, she smiled and said, 'Well now, that's a straightforward set of directions if I've ever heard one. Seems to me you have a talent for putting things into a straight line wherever possible.'

To be fair, by now I was warming to the woman, so I said it was strange that she should mention that because straight lines and square corners have always pleased me ever since I set up my first home in Swansea. You could say it has been my watchword throughout my married life. She then said, out of the blue, 'Does that apply in all that you do or just your craft work?' Well, I couldn't help saying that I have been known to turn out a tidy quilt or two and every single one of them is as straight as the day is long. My quilting squares are so accurate my husband says that you could use them to mark the footings out on a new build estate. She pressed me further, 'I can see how you could keep the blocks square so to speak on a baby's quilt but what about a full-size cover for a double bed?' Well, I thought, how does she know so much about my favourite pastime? I said to her that I always work outwards from the corner of a table following both edges then the quilt will take care of itself. Now here's the interesting bit, she said it was nice to bump into a craft-minded woman like herself. So she confirmed that she knew a thing or two

141

about quilting matters. Then she just turned and said time waits for no one just like she had said to Joan there and thanked me for pointing out the way to the station. I watched her cross the road and walk smartly up past Haggar's Cinema."

Beryl stopped and looked straight at me. "I was happy to consider my meeting with her as one of life's nice surprises, but Joan has made me think. Because it's the only topic of conversation in our house, I couldn't help but use the new builds across the town as an example. She didn't bat an eyelid you see, but I'm beginning to think now she was from the Welsh Planning office, using me to check up on my husband's paperwork.

As she sat down, I said. "Seeing as our visitor asked Beryl the way to the railway station, it won't come as a surprise to you all that the next report we'll have is from Megan."

***

Megan the Signals was on her feet before I could finish her introduction. I could see she was very keen to give us the details of her visitation from Mrs Pearl-Set.

"She must have arrived on the down train and was hanging about on the platform. I couldn't miss her. I happened to be on the way back from taking a pack of fresh corned beef sandwiches over to the signal box for my husband. Saturday is normally a reduced timetable but with all the troops arriving to go down to Castlemartin ranges for their tank training, it was more like a weekday. She was wearing a blazer and a pleated skirt, more to the point very few women in Pembroke own a blazer never mind wear one, so it was plain to me she had to be from up the line.

She asked me where the undertakers were to which I replied, I'm sorry for your loss, had they been ill very long? She smiled at me. Joan is right to say she has a lovely face on her, dimples and all. She said it was to do with a much happier event than someone passing on to the other side. I told her to go to the other end of town, turn down to the Mill Bridge where the parlour and workshop are down on the Quay.

She asked me why the trains were busy on a Saturday and I explained about the troops and told her that they would travel onward

142

in a War Department bus. Much to my surprise, she suggested that the soldiers who have disembarked at Pembroke could have marched down to Castlemartin. Then again, she said it's a good seven miles so they would have to be wearing decent socks inside their boots. She lifted her skirt a bit to show me her ankle socks saying these wouldn't be up to it, would they? I wondered for a minute if this woman had escaped from the secure hospital over at St David's but you can't be rude to visitors, can you? I said that socks, particularly army issue would have been made for comfort, not appearances.

I didn't know what to think when she asked me if I had ever knitted a pair of heavy-duty socks. I blurted out that it was one of my favourite pursuits and that if the tension of the wool across all three needles is constant then a comfortable fit could be expected. She finished off our very odd exchange by saying that if equal attention is paid to the spacing of every single stitch on each of the four knitting needles, then however complicated the pattern of the sock it would provide a lifetime of service.

Now Joan and Beryl have made me worry. I'm beginning to think that Mrs Pearl-Set was a British Rail inspector who came down on Saturday to see how our station was coping with the extra traffic. Not to mention my poor husband cooped up in the signal box pulling levers like a madman right through the day."

Megan sat down, just as confused as the rest of us.

I thanked Megan. "Well that's three occupations Mrs Pearl-Set has the credentials for, I doubt if she's blessed with more hours in the week than we all are, so she's probably none of them."

I was trying to remember where Mrs Pearl-Set had asked Megan for directions to, when Myvvi the Dead's hand went up. "You haven't heard what happened to me this morning. I can confirm that she isn't any of the things you've thought she was!"

That stopped us all in our tracks. If you had dropped a second knitting needle on a carpeted floor you would have heard it.

***

Myvvi stood and looked at several cards on which I could see she had written some notes. I caught a glimpse of the back which was

143

clearly an order of service for the celebration of the life of a recently departed mortal. As the undertaker's wife, Myvvi would find a purpose for any such leftover accessory, always discounting the cost from the bill. She always said that the family had already paid enough through the loss of their nearest and dearest.

"I was working outside the funeral workshop earlier today, down on the Town Quay, under the small lean-to built by my husband. Sometimes we are so full up with the departed that our polishing and the like has to be done out on the Quay. The locals take no notice of the coffins. Mind you, some of the naughtier boys from the Green estate have been seen climbing into one, laying down and shouting 'Ready when you are' much to the amusement of passers-by. Where was I? Oh yes, I was giving three of our luxury oak and beech coffins their final polish when the lady at the centre of all these goings-on walked up to me. She asked me for detailed directions to where we are now … St Michael's church hall. She then went on to say how much she admired the silk linings inside our top-of-the-range coffins."

I thought at this point Myvvi could have taken that bit out of her report. This was no time for a quick advertisement such that she puts in the Western Mail underneath the death notices.

Myvvi was still delivering her account. "She asked me if I had worked with other silks in our line of work to which I said our parlour had gained a reputation for exquisite embroidery on the shrouds carefully draped around the loved ones entrusted to us. She asked if I had any examples to hand. I popped in to get a few from the parlour. She was suitably impressed with the first verse of 'Calon Lan' which I'd embroidered on a royal blue shroud for a late member of the County choir. No stitch is too small for us I told her.

When I showed her the other shroud carrying a red dragon standing on two lawn bowls, she gasped out loud. I said that we respect every wish of the departed as well as those left in grief. On this occasion, they wanted to include his two favourite bowls sets to be interred with him. We might have to pay out for an additional bearer to get him up the chapel steps but no matter."

I had to force out a cough to bring Myvvi back into the realms of reality.

144

She smiled as if she was going to do just that. "Mrs Pearl-Set looked at the three coffins under the lean-two and ran a finger down the top of the one nearest to her. She then looked up at the corrugated tin roof saying to me, 'It wouldn't do to get these works of art wet, would it?' She then said she hoped that she would bump into me again and went up the Dark Lane and turned right in the direction of the Cromwell Tea rooms. I had wondered if she was from the building controls department at the Town Hall and if we would be getting a notice to take down our unapproved lean-to. Seems to me though, that our lady visitor knows far too much about our sewing circle for comfort. The question we should all be asking is who amongst us can shed any real light on the true identity of Mrs Pearl-Set?"

Myvvi collected her service cards from the table and sat down.

Bessie pushed her chair back and said. "It's plain to me that this is a mystery which should not be continued any further." She turned and walked over to the door leading to the entrance porch. We all heard her say. "Ah, there you are Lily, you found us. Mind you, we're all capable of giving you clear directions as you've been finding out this past week."

***

Bessie collected a chair from the stack by the wall and invited her guest to sit alongside her. Our visitor was wearing a pale yellow twin-set and her now expected if not compulsory pearls, complete with that lovely smile of hers.

Bessie couldn't hold back, she was grinning from here to Pembroke Dock. "This is Lily Jones, the application officer of the Welsh National Guild of Craftswomen."

Lily looked around the circle and smiled briefly at all present but nicely at the four of us who had already met her. Fortunately, most of our open mouths had been closed by now.

Bessie went on. "There is so much good work going on in our group that I thought it was about time that we threw off our shackles of modesty so to speak and brought our activities to the attention of the appropriate authorities."

My mind was spinning. Why on earth would Bessie even think

145

about exposing our undercover efforts to keep our town tidy and safe? I needn't have worried.

Bessie turned to Lily saying. "You have been handling our application to be recognised for our handicraft skills not to mention conducting the personal interviews which are part of the proceedings. Would you like to let us know how we've measured up to your standards?"

Lily stood up, her relaxed stance told me that she was used to addressing a bewildered gathering. "First of all, I would like to apologise to everyone for the secrecy attached to my work over the past week in Pembroke. In particular, to the four ladies I've met who Bessie had said were the very essence of all that you do here. I dare say between you, I have been acclaimed as a local government inspector all the way up, or even down depending on your preferences, to be the next prospective candidate for the Pembrokeshire constituency. In the past, the one suggestion I wasn't that keen on, was the time I had to visit a small village outside Builth Wells. I was accused of being a spy working for Whitehall who wanted to make the Welsh language an optional extra to English in the local secondary school!"

There were a few smiles around the table, we've had our version of English in South Pembrokeshire since the Normans and their Flemish tradesmen built our castle eight hundred years ago.

Lily carried on. "It's only when we have examined your craftwork and talked to your members that we are able to award you the membership of our exclusive guild. There have been I have to say instances where the reputation of a group has exceeded their capabilities. In those circumstances, I endeavour to ensure that the proposer is the only person who has to deal with the disappointment."

She took a sheet of paper from her handbag and turned to Bessie. "I'm delighted to inform you, that there is no such disappointment coming your way." Her voice became more animated. "I today have approved the appointment of the Station Road Sewing Circle to the Welsh National Guild of Craftswomen."

Bessie's face was a picture, she was beaming with pride. A roar went up, Bron the Books and Penny the Photo were on their feet and dancing like a pair of fools. The celebration went on for ages. When Bessie finally called us all to order by announcing that it was time to sample the cream slices and apple turnovers in the kitchen, fresh from Hall the Bakers, I decided to apologise to our guest and give her some recognition for herself. I walked over and said. "You'll have to pardon my behaviour when we first met, you'll always be welcome here in Pembroke. We will all look fondly back on this week as the time that we first met up with Lily the Guild."

She smiled. "I'll treasure that tally for sure. I hope very much that this will be the start of a long relationship which will encourage anyone with a craft or indeed any talent in Pembroke to put it to its best possible use."

I couldn't help myself. "Don't you worry about that girl, the vital work going on in this sewing circle will go on as long as any of us are still breathing!"

The End

Ingram Content Group UK Ltd.
Milton Keynes UK
UKHW021955200723
425516UK00013B/368